INTRODUCTION

My life was meant to change when we escaped our past.

New family. New town. New school.

I find myself living in a shinier version of hell, with a devil hell bent on crushing me.

My new stepbrother, the heir to the Knight fortune and legacy, is also my senior year English teacher. He doesn't hold back on punishing me in class.

The three Kings that rule St. Ivy and this town have also set their sights on me. Specifically, one who seems to have a personal vendetta against me. His callous gaze, wrathful mouth, and vengeful ways know no bounds.

His two devious best friends are no saints, with their irresistible smirks and flirty touches, some bordering on the line of possessive.

Little do they know I made a promise to myself long ago that I would never again be a possession.

They seem to think they can break me.

But these boys don't know who they're dealing with. I've faced monsters that would make them hide under their beds and piss in their pants. Monsters who taught me to put up impenetrable shields to keep me safe inside.

The irresistible torture of these manipulative Kings has me fighting my own demons.

I manage to resist the four of them until my walls slowly crack, my truths start spilling out, and my past comes crashing into my present.

CHAPTER ONE

Peyton

They say when life gives you limes, drink tequila shots. No, that's not quite right, but at this point what else did I have to fucking lose? I pulled my long hair back out of my face, bent down, and licked the salt off her tanned skin just above her G-string. Then I slurped up the tequila from her navel. I moved quickly to suck the lime from her mouth as the already drunk crowd hollered and whistled with excitement at seeing two senior girls locking lips. Fucking immature imbeciles.

The tequila burned its way down my throat. The salt on my tongue did nothing to ease the acid feeling, and the lime was as sour as shit, making me almost gag at the aftertaste.

"Fuck yes." Eli pressed against my ass and wrapped his muscled arms around my waist as he lifted me off the ground and twirled me around in the air.

I watched the senior student body as I was spun around, all packed into the Boat House, having one last party before senior year started on Monday. Most of them freshly returned from spending their summer holidaying in their parent's houses in Europe. You could tell the ones who stayed here in Boat Harbor, their deep summer glow visible on all their exposed skin. I barely knew any of them, but I had memorized the faces I needed to steer clear of and the queen bee I was supposed to fear.

Eli placed me back on my feet and kissed the side of my head in a show of ownership of sorts. Only, we weren't together, and I had never given him the impression I was interested in him or any of the guys in this preppy seaside town. The small gesture got the attention of Steele, one of the kings who ruled this place. If you didn't know the two of them personally, you'd think they were brothers. Both had the tell-tale signs of living by the ocean, with their deeply tanned skin and sun-bleached, messy hair. The thing that set them apart was the cerulean blue of Steele's eyes compared to Eli's hazel ones. And their polar opposite personalities. Eli's fun and easygoing nature was overshadowed by Steele's ever-present murderous glare. Steele looked like he'd mow down your kitten if it got in his way.

I watched Steele's hostile gaze as it settled on me, his face a mask of annoyance as his full lips set into a scowl. I hadn't spoken a word to him since moving here, so I had no fucking idea why he was so spiteful and why he went out of his way to avoid me like the plague.

"Ty got the good shit. Want to come share?" Eli whispered in my ear.

"No thanks. You know I don't do that." I twisted to look up at him. His already drunk ass made his eyes glassy. I grinned at him and his lopsided smile.

"Don't leave without me." He planted

another kiss on my cheek before he jumped on Ty's back. The two of them scurried off into one of the back conference rooms as a group of senior boys trailed after them.

Tyler, or Ty, as everyone liked to call him, was another member of the pack. There were three of them. Steele, Tyler, and Hawke. They ruled the halls of St. Ivy as well as all of Boat Harbor. Their families dated back generations in this town, owned most of it, and ruled it with their old money.

My skin prickled, and the feeling of being watched had me scanning the room. An uneasy feeling had settled in my stomach, a feeling I hadn't felt in a while. My eyes connected with Steele again, and I could feel his malevolence from across the room. It radiated in waves of malice and contempt. His tall, muscular frame towered over the other students, and his muscles bulged against his plain black t-shirt. I allowed my eyes to roam his face and take in all his beauty. His sun-bleached hair sat in a wavy mess and framed his piercing eyes. A cigarette hung at the corner of his mouth; the smoke circled in mesmerizing patterns above him. My eyes were drawn to his hands, where he flicked a switchblade open and closed between his fingers. He didn't bother to look at the sharp blade as it moved nimbly in his fingers. He simply kept his dark gaze on me.

I stared at him for what felt like an eternity. The rest of the crowd faded into the background as we sized each other up. Neither of us wanted to back down first. His cold stare washed over me like a bucket of ice had been poured over my head, the feeling both chilling and exhilarating. Some idiot bumped into me, making me break my eye contact as I steadied myself from falling. I was relieved that our stare down was over, but some part of me felt like Steele had won an unknown game. It didn't sit well in my gut, and I stole one more glance at him before I turned on the spot and exited the main room. I wasn't going to put up with this shit this year. I was here for one thing; to finish my senior year and get the fuck as far away from the east coast as I possibly could, leaving behind a childhood full of torture and bad memories and making sure no one remembered the name Peyton Murdoch.

I moved through the crowd with ease and

made my way outside to the back deck, which overlooked the ocean. This beach house had sat in this spot since the beginning, having been built by the founding fathers and passed down through the generations of Boat Harbor. A legacy of the town. It was now called the Boat House, where the rich locals met for lazy lunches and golfed all weekend.

Boat Harbor was nestled against the sharp cliffs to the north and the sandy white beaches to the south. It was steeped in rich history and clouded in dark secrets, ruled by the four families who owned pretty much everything in town. And most importantly, it was far enough away that no one would know who my mom and I were. Far enough away that the monsters wouldn't search this far south for us.

The ocean breeze swirled around me as the waves crashed against the shore under the iridescent glow of the full moon. In the distance, I could make out the dotted lights of the center of town. Their twinkled display reminded me I had to get school supplies. I groaned internally as I made my way down the weathered steps and onto the beach. I pulled my sandals off to feel the cool sand between my toes as I headed straight for the water, the waves beckoning me and teasing me to dip my feet in.

The water was like ice against my hot skin, and I marveled at the instant calm that washed through me. I waded in further until the waves lapped at my knees, and I closed my eyes. I could hear the loud booming music from the party and the faint shrieks of others further down the otherwise deserted beach.

An icy male voice brushed against my exposed skin. "Careful, Knight, you don't want to drown."

I jumped and spun around. I had been so wrapped up in my thoughts that I hadn't heard him approach. From the glow of the moonlight, I could just make out his face as he waded into the water to tower over me.

"I'm not a Knight." I glared at him.

Steele Manning stood about a foot away from me, his 6'6 muscled frame blocking the view of the Boat House behind him. His hands were lazily placed in his pockets as though he didn't have a care in the world. Rich boys like him didn't need to have a care in the world.

Their wants and desires were handed to them on a silver platter, all paid for by daddy, dearest.

"No, Princess, you'll never actually be a Knight. As much as you try." His eyes raked over me, trailing from my lips down to where the sea water met my knees and back up. A look of disgust washed over his perfect features.

My anger started to burn through me. "Are you done ogling, big boy?"

He stepped closer and his stomach brushed my breasts. But I didn't move. I wasn't about to let this asshole intimidate me. His ocean blue eyes brewed a storm in them, making his face grow darker under the moonlight. I could see he was churning something over in that pretty head of his, and he wasn't about to let me leave until he told me exactly what he needed.

"I don't ogle lower class sluts." He cocked his head to the side. His arrogance rolled off him, and I could feel him chuckle against me, each movement sending heat to my skin.

I felt his insult to my core. "Well, lucky me then." I stepped back, but a wave crashed against my legs, and I fell into him. My hands gripped his t-shirt as his arm snaked around my waist and held me firmly against him.

"Already throwing yourself at the king and we're not even at school yet." He pulled me harder against him as his fingers dug into my waist to the point of pain.

"Get over yourself." I pushed myself away and started to move out of the water.

"Not so fast, ice queen."

I was jerked to a stop by his grip on a fistful of my hair. I turned to face him again, wincing at the pain radiating through my scalp. This time, the moon's glow illuminated his features, his sharp jaw and lips on full display. He looked like a god, and he fucking knew it.

A strand of my hair was still held firm between his fingers. "Let go," I gritted through my teeth as I stepped closer to him, my knuckles straining under my clenched fists.

"Is this white-blond natural or box dye?" He dropped the strand of my hair like it would give him a disease and rested his eyes on me.

My breath caught in my throat, and I tried not to let him see I was affected by his assholery. "None of your fucking business." I flipped him the finger.

Steele paused, eerily calm as he glared at me. "Now that I have your attention. If you know what's good for you, you'll steer clear of St. Ivy."

"Unlucky for you, I don't give a fuck, rich boy." I purposely barged my shoulder into his ribs as I stormed past him. He barely moved from the impact, and that pissed me off even more.

His hand snapped out and grabbed me by the elbow, jerking me closer to him. I lifted my chin as I stared up at him, his earthy cologne overwhelming me. His hand on my skin felt like fire, and my stomach tied in knots.

He narrowed his eyes and licked his lips. "If you come to school on Monday, I'll make your life not worth living."

"Oh yeah, don't make promises you can't keep." I tried to rip my arm free, but his grip only tightened. His eyes changed to a deep blue as the rage in him swirled.

I had no clue as to why he was being such a prick to me, but I guessed it was his way of feeling important. Pick on the new girl, make the school think you're still a god. Wanker.

"I promise to break you, Knight." Steele's voice dripped with venom, and I didn't doubt he'd try his best to break me. Only, I was so fucking broken already, nothing he could do would rattle me.

"I look forward to it," I lied. I had no inclinations to fight a war I knew I wouldn't win. Not in this town, with these savage kings who ruled the school. They had back up in spades, and I only had my mom.

Steele's eyes searched mine as though he couldn't work me out. I doubted anyone had challenged him before, let alone a girl. He held my gaze, and his mouth turned into a sinister smirk before his head snapped up and he looked behind me. "Looks like you're getting rescued from the big bad wolf."

"I don't need rescuing," I spat and turned my head to see Eli headed toward us. His eyes were cautious as he glanced between Steele and me.

"Are you okay, Peyton?" Eli stopped a good few feet away from us, and I noticed Steele and I were still flush against each other.

It would have looked like a totally different scenario from where Eli stood and a small part of me hoped this would make Eli back off a bit.

"She's perfect. Aren't you, princess?" Steele glanced back down at me and demanded my attention with a squeeze of my arm.

"I'm fine." I snaked my free hand under Steele's shirt and pinched his smooth skin between my fingernails. It didn't have the effect I'd hoped for; he barely even moved. Steele growled low and deep in his chest before he let my arm go.

He leaned down so his face was close to mine and whispered so only I could hear, "Your funeral."

I wanted to punch Steele's perfectly sculpted face, but I took the high road and stormed back up to the party. Fuck him. Fuck them all. I wasn't going to let a group of over privileged teenage boys get under my skin. I had one year to deal with, then I was out of here. I'd keep my head down and focus on my grades, attend classes and that's it. No extra-curricular activities, and I wasn't going to let Capri convince me to attend one of these stupid parties again. When I finally left this preppy town, it would be as though I never existed in the first place.

CHAPTER TWO

Peyton

"Peyton, get your ass up!"

"Go away." I groaned as I checked my phone for the time. Fuck. I scrambled out of bed and straight into my bathroom.

Perks of living in this house with my new stepdad and sister was that we kids got our own wing, each room had a bathroom, sitting area and a balcony that overlooked the ocean. This house was a monster of a house, three levels of pure, whitewashed Hamptons beauty with manicured gardens and a pool house right on the beach. Our old home was not small in comparison, but it lacked the warmth and family vibes this Knight mansion exuded. My old home was made of dark enemies and dodgy money.

Mom and I moved to this town months ago. We laid low, and I was home schooled for the remainder of junior year. Mom met Nathaniel Knight during a business conference, and the rest was history. I was happy for her; he treated her right and he'd shown me nothing but kindness and treated me the same as his own flesh and blood. Well, the kid I had met so far. My stepsister, Capri Knight, was like a long-lost sister. We hit it off from the get-go and will finish senior year together at St. Ivy Prep. I hadn't met my stepbrother yet; he left Boat Harbor straight after high school to go to college a few years back and hadn't yet returned.

The weird thing about this house was that there were no photos of Capri or my stepbrother displayed anywhere, not even a baby photo. Mom always had photos of me and her and even my dickhead dad in picture frames throughout our old house. All those pictures now sat neatly packed up inside boxes in storage along with the rest of our past.

After my quick shower, I blow-dried my waist-length icy blonde hair into loose curls, applied my make-up, and headed for my walk-in. My ugly ass uniform stared back at me. Did kids really dress like this? Was this some sort of joke at my expense? I ran my hand over the dark blue plaid skirt and fingered the embroidered school emblem on my blazer. Begrudgingly, I got dressed and sat on my bed to pull my knee-high socks up when Capri stormed in.

"Come on, breakfast is waiting." She clapped her hands at me.

I slipped my feet into my platform Mary Janes and fastened the buckles. I stood up and twirled in front of Capri. "Do I pass for a St. Ivy snob?" I grinned.

Capri whistled and said, "Those boys won't know what hit them." She eyed me up and down.

"I don't have the time or patience for boys this year," I scoffed, grabbing my school bag, and following Capri downstairs.

Mom and Nathaniel were already seated at

the breakfast bar, deep in conversation. My heart swelled at the sight. I hadn't seen my mom and that bastard called my dad like this, ever. Mom glanced up and looked like she was about to cry but managed to hold herself together.

"You two look cute. Stand there and let me get a photo." She pointed at the large bay window overlooking the lush green gardens.

"Mom." I rolled my eyes but did as she asked.

Capri linked her arm through mine and kissed me on the cheek as my mom took the photo. "Don't worry, Nicki, I'll take good care of her today," Capri reassured my mom.

"Thanks, sweetheart," Mom replied, sitting back down in her chair.

I parked myself at the end of the island bench and stared at breakfast. I couldn't stomach food this early and with the nerves that somersaulted in my gut, I doubted I'd keep anything down.

Nathaniel smiled at me. "There's freshly brewed coffee in the pot."

"Thanks." I grinned back, happy that he understood how I felt.

He added, "Don't be nervous today. Most of the kids at the school are friendly."

"Most?" I quirked a brow.

"Well, you know what high school can be like." He winked at me as though he joked a warning.

"I'll keep an eye out for the unfriendly ones, thanks." My stomach dropped at the thought. I was in no mood to deal with dickheads today. My period was ravaging my uterus and I was bloated as fuck. Safe to say I was a moody bitch.

"I'll drive," Capri announced, jumping off her chair. Her enthusiasm to get to school was comical. I knew exactly the reason for her sudden need to be extra early. It had to do with a certain lacrosse captain she couldn't detach herself from at the party on Friday night. I managed to cover for her and her all-nighter with Mr. Dreamboat.

I was glad Capri offered to drive. My Maserati was left behind, and up until now, I had no use for a new one seeing as I was home schooled. Plus, Mom was funny with giving our names and details out to root us to one place. She was overly cautious when it came to me, and I had to beg and plead with her to let me go to an actual school for senior year. With the encouragement of Nathaniel and Capri, we managed to wear her down until she agreed.

"Have fun, girls," Mom called after us, and I could sense the worry in her tone.

We climbed into Capri's sleek black Mercedes, and my anxiety hit my throat as she took off down the long driveway. I watched the azure blue of the ocean water as we drove along our street. It looked so inviting, and I had a sudden urge to take up mom on her offer to home-school me. At least that way I had the option to go for late morning swims and do schoolwork until early evenings. I started to second guess my need to attend school on campus, but it was too late now. I had committed, and I was no quitter.

Capri parked the car in the lower parking lot reserved for students, and I eyed the groups of uniforms as they hovered around their obscenely expensive cars. Everyone looked the same. My old school, although private and exclusive, was much more lenient on the uniform policy. This school was next level.

"Ready?" Capri grabbed my hand and squeezed it. She seemed to sense when things became too much for me.

I glanced at her and her perfectly straight hair. She was stunning, to say the least, even with this new hair color that had gone wrong. It was supposed to turn out a honey color, not a vibrant, burnt copper. "Nope." I shook my head in response. My nerves chewed my insides and made my stomach feel like it was getting punched from the inside out.

She replied, "You'll be fine. If we have no classes together, I'll show you where we eat lunch." Capri leaned over the seat and grabbed her bag before climbing out.

"Here goes nothing," I said to myself as I grabbed the strap of my bag and hauled my ass out of the car.

I could feel all eyes on me as I followed Capri out of the parking lot and up the stairs. I'd met a few of the students during the summer break, but it was in passing, nothing to write home about. Apart from Capri's friends, along with Eli and his mates, I didn't know anyone here. As we reached the top of the stairs, my breath caught in my lungs. St. Ivy was a sight to behold. Its gothic architecture sat heavy in this vibrant and bright seaside town. The dark brick buildings with their towers loomed over the estate and made it feel as though Count Dracula himself roamed the halls after dark.

I quickened my steps and followed Capri, who was set on getting me sorted so she could meet up with her new man. The judgy looks and the whispered comments bounced off the walls as we made our way down the hall of the main building. I ignored them as best I could, but even I would have talked about me behind my back. The new girl and her mom shacked up with one of the elite families of this town. I knew what it looked like. But it was far from the truth, and I wished I could tell every one of these students to fuck off and mind their own business.

"That through there is the dining hall. I usually sit at the far table in the back corner, closest to the exit," Capri explained.

I nodded and pretended as though I'd remember where the dining hall was in this labyrinth of a school. There were buildings for each subject, buildings for gymnastics and a sports hall, and an indoor pool. To top it off the library was three stories high. I studied the map I had and tried to work out the layout of the school. It seemed simple enough on paper, with a piazza in the center of the school and the buildings dotted around the square in a pentagonal shape.

We entered the office, and Capri pushed in front of several juniors to get to the front of the line. I looked back at them apologetically, but they all seemed to know their place in the pecking order. It seemed as though seniors had the right of way at this school.

"Here's your timetable." Capri turned to me and handed me the freshly printed paper.

"How?" I started but she interrupted me.

"Hand me your map." She proceeded to exit the office with me on her heels. This girl was always in full-speed mode.

I watched as she circled parts of the buildings and drew arrows and scrawled numbers all over my map before she handed it back to me with a giant accomplished grin on her beautiful face.

"So, the numbers are the classes you have today, in order of when you have them. The arrows are the quickest way to get from one building to the next, as the entry doors don't all face the piazza, and the circled parts of the buildings are where the classrooms are located. Got it?" She beamed.

"You're insane." I laughed. "But thanks. This will be a huge help."

"We have extension math and chemistry together. Those are the last two classes. So, I'll meet you for first break here." She put the pen in her mouth and pulled the lid off before she leaned over and scribbled a love heart on the map.

"Okay." I stared at the map and wondered if it was upside down or not. I had no sense of direction so this should be an interesting first couple of days.

She batted her eyelashes at me. "Are you sure I can leave you and find my hottie?"

"Absolutely, I'll be fine. It's not the first time I'm a new student. Go, and make sure you tell me all the sloppy details." I waggled my eyebrows at her and sent her on her way.

Capri turned before she got to the end of the hall. "The lockers are down there." She pointed to a long hallway that veered to the left.

I glanced at my timetable and saw my locker

number printed at the top. So, I decided to go dump some of my notebooks in there and check out my surroundings before class started. A few students nodded and said hi as I made my way down the dark, wood-lined halls. These hallways looked as though they were plucked from some medieval castle in England. The lockers were not what I expected. Instead of the usual metal eyesore, these were beautiful carved wooden doors with the number of the locker burned into the wood. I eyed the groups of students as they chatted and laughed, all so easy and familiar. I knew what I had signed up for; the awkward and uncomfortable first few days until I found my tribe. I missed my old friends from back home. I missed my old school and the option to wear casual clothing. These skirts and pristine white shirts were too stiff and suffocating.

My eyes locked onto Hawke and Tyler further down the hall. They looked as though they were in a private, heated moment. Tyler leaned against his locker as Hawke stood inches away from him with Tyler's tie twirled in his fingers. Both guys looked at ease, but I couldn't help wondering what they were talking about. I took in all of Hawke's 6'5 frame as he leaned in and stared at Tyler. His broad shoulders filled out his school blazer and his chocolate hued hair sat in a mess of curls, still damp from his morning surf.

Tyler's icy gray gaze caught mine and he raised his eyebrow and winked at me, followed by a wicked smirk. I rolled my eyes at him and turned on the spot to face the lockers to my left. Lucky for me, it was right where mine was located. My heart raced in my chest for no goddamn reason as I fumbled and pressed the number into the key lock, hoping to all hell Tyler and Hawke stayed where they were. I did not need the attention of those assholes.

I felt the air around me pause as I slowly opened the heavy door to my locker, and I fully expected some form of prank to jump out at me or coat me in something disgusting. My locker was empty apart from one lonely card tacked at eye level. I reached in and pulled it off. Written in cursive pink letters was *Gratissimum ad infernis.*

I flipped it over, finding an emblem embossed into the thick paper, a pink skull wearing a crown with vines around it. I stared at the words and tried to recall my knowledge of Latin, but I was coming up blank.

"How sweet, you got your first love letter." Steele's chest pressed against my back, and his warmth tingled my skin.

The last thing I wanted on my first day was to face this tyrant. His long fingers snatched the note out of my hand before I could push him away. I turned in the small space between us and glared up at his baby blues. As much as I disliked the guy, I wasn't blind, and I was momentarily under the spell of his smoldering glare. He grinned down at me like a maniac, pleased to know he affected me.

His hand reached up to brush my hair back or more likely to grip my throat in warning but before he could carry out his little dominant act, I slapped his hand away. "Don't touch me."

A gasp of shock whispered through the hall, and I felt the eyes of the other students on us. I doubted anyone ever slapped any of these guys, and I had a feeling I had just started something I didn't want to be a part of. Steele wouldn't let this go. He wasn't the kind of guy to let shit like this slide and no doubt would keep his word to make my life not worth living.

"Feisty." He laughed in my face and leaned his tall frame down, so he was at eye level with me. "Don't worry, baby doll, no one is going to touch you here." His hand slid between my legs, and he pressed his switchblade against my panties.

I jerked at his touch and swung my fist towards his face, only to be stopped mid-punch by his free hand.

Steele's two sidekicks decided it was their business to join in on this little charade. Both stood on either side of the king himself, and formed a sort of barricade to the other students. Hawke grabbed my free arm in his strong fingers and held me still. My eyes snapped to his furiously dark gaze. Only snapping back to Steele when he spoke again.

"And no one is going to touch you here." Steele's eyes remained on mine as his blade trailed up my stomach and over my hardened nipple. Thank fuck I had a padded bra on because I didn't need this sick fuck knowing he was affecting me.

His blade continued up over my collarbone.

In one swift motion he had concealed it in his blazer pocket. His hand then snaked out to grab my throat, and he squeezed in warning. His eyes glimmered as he watched me stare back at him.

"And no one is going to touch you here." He moved his thumb and brushed it over my lips.

I froze at the pressure of his light touch. I went into survival mode and didn't dare move as a sickening cold shiver washed over my skin. I wanted to lash out and scream and kick at them to get them the fuck away from me, but I couldn't move. I was paralyzed and numb to the noises and movements around me. I made sure to keep my eyes locked on Steele's to ground myself in the present. I just had to concentrate on him and his blue eyes until the moment passed.

Hawke's voice dragged me back to reality. "Like a baby deer in headlights."

"A fucking adorable one at that," Ty chimed in.

But I didn't tear my gaze from Steele's as he studied me like I was a science experiment. I could see his thoughts as they swirled through him and masked his hatred for me. His touch eased from my throat, and he cocked his head to the side. His eyes moved from left to right as he tried to figure me out.

My arms were freed from both their grips when they were satisfied I wasn't going to lash out. I let out a breath as Steele straightened and dropped his hand from my neck, giving me much-needed breathing space.

"Not going to fight me, hey?" Steele grabbed my tie and tapped me on the nose.

I managed to find my voice and yanked my tie back. "You're not worth it."

"You best run along now. Wouldn't want to be late for class." Ty moved out of the way and gestured for me to escape through the gap.

I gazed around to find that all the students had disappeared, already in their first class for the day. "Move." I shoved at Steele and stormed past the three of them, unsure of where exactly I was headed.

"English lit is that way, Bambi." Hawke pointed in the other direction.

"Fuck." I groaned and turned on the spot to face them, my fists clenched in anger.

"Swearing gets you detention at St. Ivy. It's not as lenient as your old stomping ground in trash river." Ty saluted me as I sashayed past them.

I flipped them the finger as I headed to class, and I didn't want to know how Hawke knew what class I had first up. I found the building easily enough, thanks to Capri and her color-coded map. I smoothed down my tie and shirt before I grabbed the door handle and sucked in a gulp of air. I opened the door slowly and slinked in, hoping the teacher didn't notice.

Fat fucking chance. His eyes popped up from his desk as soon as I stepped a foot in.

CHAPTER THREE

Peyton

Holy fucking shit! It should be illegal for teachers to be that hot. I stood in the doorway like a fucking moron with my mouth agape before he cleared his throat and gestured for me to sit. A look of disappointment was plastered on his perfectly sculpted face as I tried to remember how to move my legs.

"If you're late again, it's detention." The annoyance in his tone rooted me to the spot. He raised his eyebrow at me and pointed to the rows of desks.

I scurried to the back of the room as other

students giggled and turned to watch me take my seat. I wanted to slide under the desk and hide for the rest of the class, but I sat there and took out my laptop, notebook and pens and pretended I didn't just get caught by the whole fucking class ogling our teacher.

Since when did a school of this caliber allow teachers to have tattoos? I'm talking a whole fucking sleeve and visible neck tatts. My mind wandered, and I caught myself thinking about what other tattoos he had hidden under his clothes. I was jolted from my thoughts when I heard my name for roll call.

"Obviously here." I waved at him and smiled innocently.

He stood from his chair and took off his black-rimmed glasses before he walked to the door and opened it. "A word outside, Miss Murdoch."

I glanced around the room, finding not one student who dared to turn around and gawk at me. I hesitated as I stared at him and stood up out of my chair. It scraped on the hardwood floors and made a terrible noise. Great, I'd probably be in detention for ruining the expensive flooring. I zigzagged through the desks and glanced up at him as I approached. He scowled back, and I instantly knew this was going to be a shit class to be in. I was barely here five minutes and I had already managed to piss the teacher off.

He followed me out the door. His chest brushed my shoulder, and I hadn't realized he was so close. I heard him close the door after us, and I stopped and turned around to wait for his words of wisdom. He was so fucking tall and muscular that I made myself look at the ground between us so I didn't get caught ogling him again.

"Miss Murdoch, eyes on me," he said in a harsh, commanding tone.

My gaze jerked up in defiance. It was a reflex I couldn't control after the torment from my past, I wasn't about to be told what to do. His eyes were the color of the ocean, a mix of turquoise and salty green, framed by thick eyebrows which were drawn together as he glared at me. He was the epitome of every school girl's wet dream. Fuck.

"Now that I have your attention, Murdoch, I do not tolerate tardiness or my student being a smartass. I'll give you leeway as it's your first class, but if you continue to disobey my rules, you and I will be spending a lot of time in detention together. Understood?" He watched me carefully, his obvious instant intolerance evident in the set of his features.

"Yes, sir." I jutted my chin out and ensured the tone of my words were understood.

He stepped closer to me, his menacing face mere inches above mine. "Don't be a little cunt," he whispered coldly.

I stared up at him, perplexed at his choice of words. Not only did he not look like a normal teacher, but he also didn't act like one either. His masculine scent swirled between us, and I tried not to let his proximity affect me. I swallowed and allowed myself to look at him, taking in his perfect features from his sharp jawline to his artfully tousled dark hair. My eyes slid to the tattoo on his neck. In cursive black scrawl was written "Love Kills" and tattooed on the other side of his neck were red lips. I watched his throat bob up and down as he swallowed and wondered who in the fuck hired this man to be a high school teacher. He didn't look much older than me, but fuck, he certainly did take on the authority role a little too enthusiastically.

"Get back into class and fucking behave," he growled in my face.

I raised my eyebrows before I purposely bumped into his arm a little harder than necessary and strode back into class to take my seat.

A few moments later, in strolled Hawke and the teacher like they had been best friends for years, chatting and laughing about some private joke. I watched them carefully as they bumped fists before Hawke made his way to one of the only two seats available. And of course, it was positioned right behind me. He winked at me and tapped my desk before he noisily seated himself in his chair.

This class had just got so much worse. I wanted to groan, but I feared it would alert Mr. Tattoos and I didn't want him to look in my direction if I could help it.

"Mr. Stryker," the teacher called from the front.

Stryker. As in Stryker Oil. Far out. Did all rich kids attend this school? I chided myself internally for not doing my homework on all the ass wipes attending St. Ivy.

"Here." Hawke kicked my chair leg, and I jerked forward.

I turned in my seat and gave Hawke my best death glare before facing the front of the class again. I gritted my teeth and waited for the teacher to start his lesson.

"Eli, take your seat." The teacher nodded at Eli as he quickly scurried to the last desk in the classroom. Why did he get a pass and was allowed to be late?

My eyes were glued to Eli as he assembled his things on his desk. His messy blonde hair was still damp from his morning surf, no doubt. He turned his attention to me and winked, not at all afraid to get caught by the asshole at the front.

The teacher cleared his throat, and my eyes snapped back to him to see his nostrils flare as his eyes slid from Eli to me and back. "Okay, welcome to senior year and all that shit. Most of you know me already from my time of reign at this school a few years back. Well, I've returned to dish out some more punishment." Mr. Tattoos chuckled and the whole class erupted into cheers and wolf whistles.

My eyes darted around the room as some of the students clapped and jumped on their seats to stomp their feet.

"Settle down. We don't want to give our new student the wrong impression of me." His eyes landed on me in a way that made my gut churn.

I glanced over at Eli as he climbed back off his chair along with the other students.

"Miss Murdoch, as a tradition in this school, I invite you to the front of the class to introduce yourself." Mr. Tattoos crossed his arms over his chest and looked smug as fuck.

I doubted this was tradition and more along the lines of his instant hatred for me.

Nevertheless, I got up out of my chair, made my way to the front of the class, and stood as far away from him as I could. "Hi everyone. I'm Peyton Murdoch, and I moved here about six months ago. I like the beach and horseback riding and getting my nails and hair done on the weekends," I said in a dumb-ass way, channeling my best Clueless impersonation. I side-eyed the teacher, hoping my dumb introduction was spot on about his preconceived thoughts on me.

I heard a faint giggle, and my eyes snapped to a raven-haired girl in the front. She winked at me, and I smiled in return, happy someone knew what I was up to.

"See me after class, Miss Murdoch." The teacher was less than amused. His striking scowl ate me up and spat me out before I could even open my mouth in astonishment.

I waltzed back to my desk with all eyes on me, including the teacher's, and came face to face with Hawke's huge shoes on my desk. "Move them before you lose them, asshole," I spat at him in anger.

He sat there and didn't move a fucking inch. He just smirked up at me like he ruled and I was to put up with his bullshit.

"Frankie, escort Miss Murdoch to the office please," the teacher commanded.

I didn't even hesitate; I grabbed my things off the desk and shoved them in my bag before I flipped Hawke the finger, and strode out of class without even a glance in the teacher's direction. Fucking asshole.

"Hey, Peyton, wait up." A melodic voice brushed against my back.

I stopped mid-stride and turned on the spot

to see the raven-haired girl as she hurried to catch up to me. "I know where the office is, you don't need to babysit me," I said, deflated. I felt bad for getting her caught up in my drama.

"Nah, it gets me out of class." She grinned and linked her arm through mine, dragging me the opposite way I was headed.

"Isn't the office that way?" I craned my neck to look behind us.

"We're not going to the office. Don't look so worried; my mom's the principal, I got this," she sang as we strode out of the building and into a darkened courtyard overgrown with vines.

I followed dubiously but allowed her to lead me to her destination. We crouched through a small opening in the thick vines and found ourselves in a densely wooded area to the back of the school. "Where are we going?" I glanced around and could barely see the blue sky through the dense canopy. The place was magical and smelled of the earth with a hint of sea spray coming in from the ocean nearby.

"To the Club House." Frankie placed her pointer finger against her lips and smiled at me.

"The Club House. Right, are we twelve or something?" I laughed. It sounded ridiculous.

She pulled me after her as we followed the well-worn path through the forest. "You'll see."

We broke free of the wooded area to come to a stop at an ancient-looking stone building. The left side closest to the cliffs was covered in moss, and I could smell the ocean thick in the air. The roar of the crashing waves against the cliffs overshadowed the whistling of the tree canopy.

Frankie stepped up to the door and pulled out her necklace, where a small bronze skull dangled in the light. I watched her lean forward and press the skull to the keypad to unlock the ancient, wooden door. If anyone wanted to get inside, they could easily kick the weathered door in; it looked as though it was about to crumble anyway.

She paused and eyed me for a moment, probably second-guessing her decision to show me this place. "Don't tell anyone I brought you here."

"Promise." I held up my hand in a scout's honor and laughed.

"You're an idiot." She shook her head and

grinned. "Follow me." She ducked through the door and held it ajar for me.

I followed her in because it was either this or going back to class with that giant dick. I glanced around at the stone walls, spotting antique lanterns that emitted a warm amber light. We had walked into a living room of sorts, decorated with chestnut colored chesterfields. It looked medieval and as though it had sat here for centuries. A narrow hallway led to a closed-door and a staircase to the right of the room lead into darkness. In the far corner was a bar stocked with endless bottles of alcohol. "Is this for the students?" I spun on the spot to see Frankie push the door closed.

"Only the special ones," she confessed before she set her sights on the bar. "Want a drink?"

"I don't drink alcohol." I followed her to the bar and placed my bag down as I climbed up on one of the stools.

She bent down and grabbed two cokes out of the fridge and handed me one. "It's still the morning, I don't drink alcohol until after dark either." She held up her coke in salute. "To making a fucking great first impression."

"Ha-ha." I tapped my can to hers and proceeded to open it. "But seriously. What the fuck is that teacher's problem?"

"Colton?" Frankie said it like I should have known his name.

"You call him by his first name?" I raised my eyebrows. Maybe this school wasn't as strict as it looked.

"He's legendary at this school, and it's his first day back since he left." Her voice was drowned out by the raucous laughter from outside.

Both our eyes snapped to the door as it opened, and in strode Tyler followed by Steele with a leggy blonde attached to his side. I knew of her. She was the queen bee of the school, the head cheerleader, and the one I was supposed to steer clear of and fear. From where I sat, she didn't look very threatening with the preppy little bounce to her step. She looked like she belonged by Steele's side, and I was glad he had someone to occupy him.

"What the fuck are you doing here, Bambi?" Tyler strode to the bar and sat his ass down next to me, way too close for comfort.

I scooted over a little and ignored him.

"No need to be scared, Bambi, I don't bite too hard." His elbow connected with my arm, and he dragged his bar stool so he had me cornered against the wall.

I glanced at him, but my eyes seemed to gravitate toward Steele. "I'm not scared of you."

The queen bee's shrill voice grated through my ears. "What the fuck is she doing here, Frankie?"

"Don't start your shit, Maddie," Frankie spat back.

I watched as Maddie peeled herself away from Steele and strode towards me, stopping beside Tyler. "Get the fuck out." She pointed to the door.

"You can't order anyone around. You're just as lowly as me and Peyton in here." Frankie crossed her arms over her chest and smirked at her.

"Steele." Maddie spun on the spot to face Steele, who simply looked bemused.

"I'm not banishing our little guest." Steele scratched his chin as his eyes landed on me. "Besides, she could put a whole new meaning to the fun we have in here." His eyes darkened at the thought.

"I'll take myself out." I jumped off the bar stool and bent down to pick up my bag, only Tyler shoved his shoe over it to stop me.

"Not so fast, Bambi." His fingers dug into my shoulder, and he hauled me back up to stand.

"Get your hands off me." I pushed at his arm and felt icy cold liquid hit me in the face.

Queen bee sneered; her satisfied grin shone like a beacon in a storm. "Go clean yourself up, skank."

I let some of the cold evil inside of me shine through my eyes as I gave her a small promising smirk. I filed the moment away, knowing I could do nothing now, but the time would come. I heard a low chuckle as I grabbed my bag and slung it over my shoulder. I sliced my eyes to Steele, finding he looked impressed by his girlfriend's efforts.

"Fucking hell, you're such a bitch." Frankie strode to the door and pulled it open before she turned to glare at Maddie. "Remember the only reason you wear the crown is because Steele still bothers to pay you attention. You will fall from your throne and land back on your ass where you belong when he's done with you. Let's go, Peyton." Frankie narrowed her eyes at Maddie.

I strode past Maddie and shoved her in the shoulder. Her petite frame nearly toppled over, only to be intercepted by Steele's wall of muscle.

"Not so fast, Knight." He crossed his arms over his chest and stared down at me.

"I'm not a fucking Knight." I stared right back into his blue eyes.

"There's payment for entering the Club House." His gaze roamed over me with a malicious glint in his eyes.

"Get over yourself." I rolled my eyes and tried to sidestep my way around him.

He flung his arm out and connected with my chest. The muscles in his forearm strained as his hand clenched into a fist. He leaned down until his lips barely touched my ear, and I felt his minty breath fan across my cheek as he whispered, "I will make you pay."

I felt the goosebumps spread across my skin when his tongue darted out and he stuck it in my ear. I jerked away from him and without a second thought, I punched him in the side of the face. "Don't fucking touch me again." I stormed to the open door and paused when I heard him chuckle.

It was a deep, perverted, and manic chuckle, one I'd associate with an escaped lunatic from an asylum. I felt the weight of his laughter as it slid across the skin on my exposed neck, as it mocked me and teased me. I didn't turn to give him the satisfaction of his effect on me and how just his existence brewed the anger and rage within. The anger and rage I tried way too hard to suppress.

I knew he would break me free. It was only a matter of time.

CHAPTER FOUR

Peyton

I had no fucking clue where Capri had disappeared to after class. One minute she was there and next she was gone. I leaned on her car and scrolled on my phone while I waited for her. Most of the cars had driven off by now and the bottom parking lot was empty apart from a few stragglers.

"Need a lift?" Eli's deep voice startled me. He stopped and leaned against the car and towered over my small frame.

I glanced up at him. He looked so fucking good in his uniform, something about his loosened tie and messy hair. "Thanks, but I'm waiting for Capri."

"She may take a while." A mischievous grin lit up his face. There was something he wasn't telling me.

"I'll wait." I shrugged.

He reached out and grabbed my tie. What was it with the guys in this school touching other people's ties? He looked torn with the words hidden just behind his lips, like any moment he would blurt them out and regret every one of them. He stepped closer, and his tall frame hovered over me, his eyes searching mine as his mouth parted to say something when we were interrupted.

A rumbling car crept up and stopped in front of us. The blacked-out windows of the sleek red Ferrari slowly opened. "Loitering on school grounds after hours is considered instant expulsion." My English teacher sneered. His narrowed eyes focused on Eli's hand as it gripped my tie before they slid to me and challenged me to dare argue.

"Leaving now, sir." Eli straightened and let go of my tie, his entire demeanor instantly changing. I knew he could feel the hatred from

Mr. Tattoos too and I wasn't just going mad.

Mr. Tattoos sped off after that, the tail of his car kicking up dirt when he left the driveway.

"What a fucktard." I stared at the dust as it swirled into the air.

"I wouldn't be saying that out loud on school grounds. Anyway, I'll catch you tomorrow." Eli hightailed it to his car in the far corner.

He waved as he drove past me, but his usual smirk was nowhere to be seen. I shrugged it off and turned to see Capri jogging toward me.

"Shit, I'm so fucking sorry, Peyton, I lost track of time," she huffed as she approached the car, her lips were puffed and reddened and her hair had signs of fingers being run through it.

"All good. I wasn't waiting for long." I winked at her.

"Let's get home and ready for the bonfire." She climbed into the driver's seat.

"Bonfire?" I got in and closed the door.

"First day of school. It's a ritual. You have to be there, seeing as you're a senior, so don't look so antisocial." Capri floored it onto the main road.

"Where's the bonfire being lit?"

"On the beach near our house." She connected her phone and let the music fill the car.

"Does the school have rituals for everything?" I rolled my eyes and stared at the ocean as we drove home. Capri kept silent for a while, not answering my question straight away and it made me think that this little town had hidden secrets that were not meant to be shared.

"Kind of. St. Ivy is steeped in weird history. There are ancient rituals carried down from the founding fathers. They were all about the elitist crap and made sure all those not involved knew about missing out." Capri finally spoke as she turned into the driveway.

"Are you fucking kidding me?" I groaned when I spotted the red Ferrari parked in front of the fountain.

"What?" Capri glanced at me and my sudden outburst.

"It doesn't even matter." I leaned my head against the headrest and hoped the Ferrari wasn't my teacher's car.

Capri edged her way to the back of the property and parked in her usual spot in the enormous garage. She climbed out and leaned back in to talk to me. "Are you coming out?"

"No, I'm staying here." I closed my eyes.

"That bad a first day, hey?" She pushed at my shoulder.

I opened my eyes and glanced at her. "You have no idea." I grabbed my bag and got out of the car.

We headed for the kitchen, where I could smell my mom's cinnamon rolls baking. It had been a ritual since I started school to have cinnamon scrolls drenched in icing as soon as I got home from my first day. We would sit and munch away while we talked. My heart swelled a little that mom even remembered to do this.

"Girl's, welcome home." Mom grinned and pointed to the bar stools for us to take a seat.

"You remembered," I said, dumping my bag and sitting down.

Capri looked between us. "Remembered what?"

"The first day of school every year, I bake rolls. They're Peyton's favorite." Mom popped a piece of a roll in her mouth.

"That's the sweetest." Capri hugged my mom.

The two of them had bonded from the very first day they met. But it wasn't hard to bond with my mom; she was the best human I knew, and Capri reminded me of her.

"Sit and I'll make some coffee before I have to go finish the rest of my work." Mom kissed Capri on the top of her head.

"We have a dinner guest tonight, so before you two skip off to the bonfire, we need you to be here for dinner," Mom said as she glanced over her shoulder.

The afternoon consisted of a Capri fashion show. She was determined to look her hottest for Jasper, the lacrosse player. I finally managed to pry his name from her after I threatened to not go to the bonfire.

"Do you think it'll be cold tonight?" She twirled and checked out her ass.

"I don't know. I've only lived here for six months." I scrolled through the music on Capri's phone.

Capri looked at me through the mirror. "What are you wearing?"

"This." I glanced down at my denim booty shorts, fishnets and my Bulls singlet.

"Umm, no to the singlet." Capri threw a

cropped black t-shirt at me with a band logo on it that I had never heard of.

"Babe, I know you don't trust easily, but trust me on this." She crossed her arms. I guessed she wasn't taking no for an answer.

"Fine, but I get to choose for you too." I climbed off her bed, swapped my singlet for her cropped t-shirt, and strolled past her into her walk-in. I grabbed out a tight dress and threw it at her. "Wear that and Jasper will drown in drool." I grinned at her.

"I didn't even know I had this." Capri held up the black dress and inspected it.

"You don't. It's mine." I laughed.

"Girls," my mom called from downstairs.

"Coming!" Capri shouted back. "I wonder who the guest is. Probably some dumb business associate with a kid hoping to get into St. Ivy." Capri rolled her eyes and quickly pulled on the dress. She grabbed my hand in hers and dragged me downstairs.

I kept pulling at the hem of the top. It was much shorter on me thanks to the size of my tits, and I felt a little uncomfortable meeting business people dressed like this. A shriek pulled me from my thoughts when Capri let go of my hand and launched herself at the guest.

"When did you get back?" she squealed.

My eyes locked with his when he set Capri back on her feet. A sly smirk turned up the corner of his lips as he took in the shock on my face.

"Oh my god, Colton, I missed you." Capri pushed at him to get his attention.

"I missed you too, sis." He kept his eyes on me.

"Do you two know each other?" Nathaniel interrupted the sibling bonding, his gaze switching from me to Colton and back.

"We were introduced this morning in class," Colton replied with an innocent smile, and I wanted to punch him in the eye.

"In class?" my mom asked, perplexed.

"He's my English teacher." I glared at him and crossed my arms over my exposed stomach.

Colton's eyes narrowed as they surveyed my crossed arms. "You've got quite the student there, Nicki."

"You're a teacher at the school? How fucking embarrassing." Capri threw her arms up in the air. "Why didn't anyone tell me?" She directed her question at her dad.

"It was supposed to be a surprise," Nathaniel huffed.

"Don't worry, I won't be bothering you." His voice rasped with an edge of anger as his eyes slid over me and connected with my glare.

"This is *my* senior year. You can't let Colton rule again. Fuck," Capri growled at her dad.

"Language," Nathaniel warned. "This is non-negotiable. Colton has done the hard yards for this."

Colton's eyes snapped to his dad. "You don't fucking say." There was an edge to his response, as though he was pissed at what he'd had to endure to get a teaching position. Fucking typical spoilt rich kid probably didn't want to work and wanted to live off daddy's money.

"Let's all go eat, shall we?" Mom, always the peacemaker, ushered Capri and I out of the formal living room.

Capri wrapped her arm around my neck and pulled me into her. "Why didn't you tell me?"

"I didn't know who the fuck he was."

"You didn't put two and two together?"

Capri glanced at me confused.

"No. He sent me to the office five minutes into class."

"The asshole." Capri let go of me and spun on the spot to head back into the formal living room.

"No, don't. Please. Please just leave it." I grabbed her hand and yanked her back into me.

"If he gives you any more shit. Let me know, okay?" She glared at Colton as he approached.

"Fine," I sighed, having no intention of following through, but knowing it would make her happy as I let her drag me into the dining room.

I slid into my seat, and to my horror, Colton decided it would be a good idea to sit to my right. He purposely bumped into me several times while he made himself comfortable. I could feel the tenseness vibrate off him and coat me. He looked calm and relaxed but the slight tightness to his jaw gave away his true feelings.

"So, Colton, what are your plans now that you're back home?" Mom tried small talk.

"I'll move into the guesthouse and continue

to work at the school until my father acknowledges I'm not fucking eighteen anymore." His voice grated against the stillness in the room.

"We are not discussing this at the table." Nathaniel matched Colton's glare and raised it.

"Well, when are we going to discuss it, father dearest? I passed your test with flying fucking colors, and you still won't let up." Colton leaned forward, braced his elbows on the table, and gripped his hands together so tight that the skull ring on his finger dug into his whitened flesh. The same skull ring that I'd seen the three dicks at school wearing, only Colton's was gold and theirs were silver.

My eyes slid to his throat, and I stared at the lips tattoo on his neck, mesmerized by the pulse of his vein under it. For some unknown reason, I had the urge to reach out and run my fingers over it to feel the strong flow of his blood under my fingertips.

"Peyton." My name jerked me back into reality.

"What?" I connected gazes with Capri, who looked back at me puzzled.

"Hurry up and eat so we can go." She motioned with her hand to scoop up my fork and eat.

"The famous first night bonfire." Colton leaned back in his seat; his mood changed as he teased Capri.

"And you're not invited," Capri retorted, shaking her head.

"You hurt my feelings, baby sis." Colton laid his large hand over his chest and pouted.

Without warning, Nathaniel stood up out of his chair and stormed off to his office, where he slammed the door shut with a wall-shaking thud.

"What's Dad's problem?" Colton looked at Capri for answers, completely oblivious to the tension his presence alone had brought to the room.

"Don't take any notice of him." My mom sighed before placing a mouthful of food in her mouth. She always turned to food to comfort herself, so I knew there was trouble in paradise. The only thing was, the trouble started today when a certain someone appeared again after being absent for three years.

Capri shot up out of her chair. "Let's go, Peyton." She held her hand out for me.

I glanced at my mom, not for permission but for a sign that she would be okay and didn't need me to stay here with her. "Go have fun." She winked at me, and a genuine smile appeared, crinkling her eyes.

I jumped out of my seat and scooted around the table, hyper-aware Colton was watching my every move, wrapping my arms around my mom's neck before kissing her on the top of her head. "I love you to Pluto and back."

"To Pluto and back, baby." She patted my hand and squeezed it to let me know she was good.

I kissed her one last time, ignored Colton as best I could, and linked hands with Capri as she dragged me out the back of the house and towards the beach.

As we passed the guest house at the far corner of the property, I couldn't help but notice the windows and doors were open. Had Colton been here for days and not let anyone know? We could have easily not noticed him, as the guest house sat right on the edge just before the dunes and overlooked the ocean. I turned and looked back up to the house and realized this position had a perfect view of my bedroom balcony. Fucking great.

CHAPTER FIVE

Peyton

I stared into the manic flames of the bonfire as they licked and danced towards the midnight sky. The faint howl of the wind circled and drowned out the shit music being blasted through the giant speakers. The heat from the flames tingled my skin. I relished in its warmth, and I realized the booty shorts and midriff top I'd worn was a dumb decision.

I looked around the beach and noticed most seniors were huddled in groups, drinking and dancing, trying to get closer to the three assholes as they sat at the top of the beach looking down their noses at everyone. Their faces were shadowed from sight as a group of wannabes hovered near them. I didn't understand the whole hierarchy of this school, or why students were so eager to be a part of it all. Sucking up to the three kings, like they were the gods of the school. As if they didn't already have it all: good looks, brains, varsity athletes, and heirs to their family's kingdoms. They also had to rule the fucking school.

I made my way down the beach towards the cliffs, happy to get away from the noise. I'd lost Capri at some point, and I figured she was off with her new man, so I didn't bother to look for her. As the noise of the bonfire faded and was taken over by the rhythmic crash of the waves, my inner anxiety slowly faded.

"Hello, sis." A husky voice broke over the sound of the waves.

I spun on the spot to come face to face with Colton, hidden in the shadows of one of the overhanging boulders. He looked so fucking good in the soft glow of the moon and every part of my body hummed with desire as much as my brain tried to stop it.

"What are you doing out here?" I dug my

toes into the soft sand to anchor myself.

"Whatever the fuck I like." His words came out hushed, and the meaning behind them was not lost on me. I knew he was capable of getting away with anything and from only a few moments I'd shared in his presence, I knew he could be a giant dick.

I raised my eyebrows. "I'll leave you to it." I turned to walk away, but his voice halted me in my tracks.

"You're not going anywhere." His words were commanding, and I wondered if he always spoke in a teacher tone.

I took a step back and studied him. He leaned against the rough rocks in his swim shorts and a t-shirt that clung to his muscled chest and arms. My eyes lingered on the sleeve of tattoos on his left arm, the bright moonlight highlighting the dark ink.

"You can come closer to get a better look." He smirked, but the humor didn't touch his broody eyes.

I snapped my eyes to his. "Why were you such a dick to me in class today?"

His gaze snaked over me and paused at the top of my thighs for a moment before they moved upwards until they met my glare. His scrutiny of me felt forbidden and impure. His face remained emotionless, but there was a hidden sadness behind his eyes, a world of buried secrets and murky half-truths threatening to escape. "Watch how you speak to me." His voice came out in a hiss.

"We're not in class right now, so I don't have to behave." I clenched my fists in frustration. Why was he such a pain in my ass?

He pushed himself off the rocks, standing at full height and staring down at me. "Oh, really. Come closer." He crooked his finger and beckoned me toward him, daring me to run.

Every part of my body warned me not to obey, but I ignored it, and like an idiot, I took a few steps toward him. My heart hammered in my chest, and my breath caught in my throat as I stared up at him. I knew I shouldn't fear him, but he gave off vibes that chilled me to the bone and stirred feelings of lust and wanting that I hadn't felt in a long time. Feelings I didn't think would surface ever again after the ordeal my dad put me through.

"So obedient." His slow and lazy smile showed his perfect row of teeth.

"Fuck you." I was brought back to reality from his words, and I spun on the spot to escape him.

His hand gripped my wrist, and he stopped me from moving. "Not so fast."

"Let go of me, or I'll fucking scream." I yanked my arm, but his fingers tightened.

"Scream all you want." His eyes glistened with excitement as they scanned my face, daring me to carry out my threat.

"What the hell is your problem?" I stopped trying to escape him and stood still.

His face turned dark; all emotion drained from his features. "You." He said it like I should have known all along. He stepped closer to me, my wrist still held firm in his grip.

I swallowed at his closeness. He felt like sin, and forbidden temptation all rolled into a perfect reason to go to hell. I tried to hide the desire in my eyes, but he looked at me like he wanted to devour me. "You don't even know me," I breathed in frustration.

"Not yet, but I plan to get to know every last bit of you," he whispered. His threat sent fear and an ache through me.

He dropped my wrist and stepped back

away from me as though he had been struck by lightning, as though he couldn't get far enough away from me. I realized why he had moved so quickly when I heard voices approaching. We stared at each other; confusion rocked my core at how he had made me feel just a moment ago.

"Peyton, what are you doing here?" Capri cocked her head to the side as she approached the overhanging rocks with her new man on her arm. Her eyes widened when she spotted Colton, half-hidden in the shadows.

"I found your brother and wanted to know why he was such a dick to me in class today." I smiled at him, and his lips curled over his teeth in a sneer.

"What are big brothers for, if not to torment their little sisters." The edge of darkness in his tone made me want to punch him.

"Colton, stop being an asshole." Capri kicked sand at him.

"Can't help myself." He chuckled. "I'll leave all you children to play nicely with each other." He brushed past me as he headed back up the beach to the house.

I watched him in the dark, his tall frame

against the white sand silhouetted by the moonlight. I couldn't work him out, and that pissed me off.

"I'm so sorry, Peyton. I'll get dad to deal with him." She linked her arm through mine and pulled me into her. "Jasper, meet Peyton, my sister. Peyton, meet Jasper." Capri's grin widened when she looked up at him.

"Hey," he said, waving awkwardly at me.

"Hi." I smiled back. He seemed like a nice guy compared to the assholes I'd managed to have run-ins with today. "You know what?" I pulled myself away from Capri. "I need a drink. Catch you two later." I winked at her, and she mouthed thanks in return as Jasper stepped forward to put a protective arm around Capri, steadying her on the soft sand.

I strolled back up to the bonfire and admired the glow from the row of mansions that sat beyond the dunes, each one different yet just as obnoxiously lavish as the next. The Knight residence sat in the center, and I watched the lights flicker off in the master on the top floor. As I made my way up the sand, the hairs on the back of my neck prickled as I approached the drinks station, and the feeling did not sit well in my gut. My senses focused on the noises around me as I kept my eyes on the selection of drinks in the various ice containers. I heard the crunch of the sand as footsteps approached me. I ignored them and kept my gaze down.

"Hey, beautiful, how about we go into the bushes, and I give you proper St. Ivy welcome?" The waft of expensive cologne mixed with alcohol surrounded me. Sweaty hands gripped my shoulders as some pretentious wanker pressed against my back and pushed his hard dick against my ass.

I froze, not wanting to draw attention to us. He took my non-answer as his cue to grip me around the waist, and I let him turn me around to face him. I knew him from school today; he was just one of the entitled jocks who thought they could take what they wanted.

"I don't fucking think so," I replied, smiling innocently.

"You know you're begging for it, slut," he slurred as he tried to kiss me.

The itch to feel the crack of his bones break under my knuckles overwhelmed me, and before I could stop myself, my fist connected with his nose. The satisfying crunch sang in my veins.

He instantly let go of me, his hands flying to his face. "You fucking psycho bitch!" he roared as the blood poured out of his nose and over his lips and chin.

I stuck my hand in one of the ice buckets to stop the swelling of my knuckles. This fucker had a hard face, and I'd be feeling the aftereffects in the morning. I stood there and watched him wipe the blood on his t-shirt before he snorted back and made the most disgusting sound. His rage-filled eyes zoned in on me, and a look of hatred coated his twisted features. Without warning, he lunged.

"What the fuck is going on?" Tyler intercepted the guy in a death grip to the throat before he could reach me. My eyes focused on Tyler's arm, the muscles straining as he held the guy at arm's length. I'd never noticed how built Tyler was; the school blazers camouflaged everything.

I had no idea where Tyler appeared from or what gave him the idea that I needed saving, but I stood back, amused at the sight of my would-be harasser as he spluttered blood all over Tyler's arm.

"I tripped and fell into the table." The guy glared at me. His hands were wrapped around Tyler's wrist. Both of us knew he had no chance of winning in a fight against Tyler, who held the title of MMA champion for his weight group three years running.

I snorted at his response and pulled my hand out of the ice just as Tyler's gaze landed on my fist. I wasn't used to guys defending my honor. Only one had ever bothered, and he was still tangled up in the mess my mom and I ran from. I pushed the thoughts of him into the back of my mind; now was not the time or place to be thinking of him or the past.

I watched Tyler's eyes snap to the guy who tried to attack me, and a torrent of pure rage flared from his nostrils as he pushed him back into the thick bushes. "Fucking touch her again and see what happens. I dare you," Tyler growled as they disappeared.

I could hear the gurgled and choked sounds of someone's airways being cut off, and I knew I should have left. But the depraved inner me stood and listened intently until I heard the guy's gasps through the bushes just as Tyler reappeared with not a hair out of place. As though he hadn't exerted any energy choking someone.

"He won't bother you again." His icy gray gaze connected with mine before it slid to my hand resting at my side.

"You didn't need to do that." I stared up at him and his perfect jawline bowed lips and messy black hair. He stood there all sexy and smoldering and I couldn't help but check him out.

"Clearly, you can take care of yourself." He gestured to my hand. "But I don't put up with rapey shit." His lips curled, and he bared his perfect row of teeth at me.

His statement confused me. Earlier today, he stood just inches from me when his best mate ran his switch blade up my skirt and over my breast in a show of who's king shit. Tyler, I decided, was a hypocrite, and I made a mental note to never trust him or his word.

I shook my head slightly in disappointment of this realization and he gave me a look. His eyes penetrated my skin as though he tried to figure out my thoughts. "We told you no one would touch your goods. No one but one of us." His dark chuckle slammed against me, and I missed his hand as it reached out and chucked me under the chin.

I shivered from the contact of his fingers. God, I was broken. I hated him and his cocky friends, even if they were hot as fuck. I turned on the spot and stormed my way back to the house.

Tomorrow was going to be a better day.

CHAPTER SIX

Peyton

Nearly two weeks passed without as much as a second glance from the three assholes, and a small part of me stayed on edge as I waited for our next run in. I'd discovered that I had at least one asshole in each of my classes, apart from study hall, and it ground my gears. I needed a break from them and their watchful eyes.

The guy with the broken nose hadn't been seen since the bonfire, and I wondered if he was laying low with his tail between his legs. Rumor had it that Tyler was choke happy and the incident at the bonfire wasn't the first.

Friday finally showed itself, and I managed to turn up ten minutes early for English; the last thing I needed was a repeat of my first Monday morning in this place. The door was already open, and Colton was seated at his desk, his eyebrows furrowing as he glared at his phone screen. He looked fucking delicious in his navy dress pants and a tight white button up shirt with the sleeves rolled up to showcase his tattooed arms. And to polish off his mouthwatering teacher look, he had motherfucking suspenders on. I took my seat, and he didn't acknowledge my presence, which was good. Maybe he'd had a change of mind and decided it was too much effort to torture me each lesson. I unpacked my laptop and notebook and pulled out my novel to read a few pages as other students started to filter in.

"Okay, class. I'll hand out the paperwork for your end of term paper. It's paired work, so I'll need you all to pick a partner." Colton cleared his throat as his eyes landed on me. A wicked smirk turned the corners of his mouth up slightly before he continued. "Peyton and

Hawke, you two will be partnered up. If I hear any complaints, you'll be in detention for the rest of the semester." He kept his dark gaze on me and waited for my objection.

I stared right back at him, and my body practically vibrated with rage. I clenched my fists together under the table and gritted my teeth until I was sure they would shatter in my mouth. Hawke kicked my chair leg and I jerked forward. I turned in my seat and gave him a fake ass smile before I turned back to face the front of the class.

"Oh Bambi, we're going to have so much fun spending time together." Hawke's words hit me in the back of the head, and made my already simmering anger almost bubble over.

"Get on with it, guys." Colton let the rest of the class pick their partners as the sheets of paper, with the task printed on it, were passed back. He had a smug as fuck look on his face and I knew he was only doing this to get under my skin.

I snatched the sheet from the person in front and stared at it. Fucking Macbeth. How fucking fitting. After a few minutes of being absorbed in reading the task information, I looked up to see Colton standing over my desk.

"Miss Murdoch, it's good to see you're on time. I thought you'd be late after your lengthy bathroom session this morning." His eyes bored into my skull and I didn't know what he planned to achieve with that statement.

I heard giggles from the other students, but I kept my eyes glued to Colton's. Fuck, were there cameras in my bathroom? Did he see me in there? The thought cooled my blood and my hand instinctively touched the area at my hip. Oh fuck. Did he know?

He didn't say another word. He simply winked at me coolly and sauntered back to his desk like an alley cat that had just caught the biggest rat on the street and was gloating to the other strays.

I sunk into my chair and hoped to fuck he didn't know my secret. No one knew, apart from Dylan, and he only found out because he barged in on me one time. I didn't allow my thoughts to linger on Dylan and my past, but I wanted to run out of the classroom and straight into the sea to let it swallow me whole. I sensed Eli's gaze on my skin, I turned to him and gave him a small, fake smile and hoped to all hell it was enough to keep him off my back.

Study material for the assignment was placed in a dingy side room at the back of the classroom, and as much as I didn't want to move from my desk, I hauled my ass up and headed to the back of the room to collect some of the materials. I narrowed my gaze at Hawke as I passed his desk, knowing fully well that I'd be doing the entire assignment myself, so I didn't have to spend any extra time in his presence.

"Fucking dumb whore, thinking Colton has any interest in you. As if you'd be so dense." A scratchy voice filled my personal space.

I counted to three before I sliced my deadly gaze to the culprit. "What the fuck did you just say?" I eyed Stass, as she placed one hand on her hip and glared back at me.

Miss big tits, with way too many shirt buttons undone, smirked at me. Obviously pleased with the attention. "Back the fuck off, bitch. He's not interested in you." She chewed her gum with an open mouth. The sound was disgusting.

I moved my gaze back to the papers in my hands and gripped them until they scrunched together. I had to control my anger, and right now this bitch was testing me. "Get the fuck out of my face before I break yours." I growled. The dumb bitch must have realized I wasn't playing because she backed the fuck up and left me alone.

I closed my eyes and breathed in and out for a count of three, enough to calm myself and not cause her any injuries. I felt heat press up behind me, blocking me against the low shelf. I knew it was him, I could tell from the way my body responded to his. His hand gently caressed down my neck and over my shoulder, causing a ripple of desire to flood through me.

I felt him shift as he leaned down to whisper in my ear. "What have I told you about that smart mouth, Peyton? Stop running it in my class or I'll find a better use for it."

I shivered, wanting to be disgusted, but all I could feel was the heat burning between my legs. I pushed back into him, teasing him as much as he was teasing me. "I'm not yours to tell what to do, Sir. I'm sure you can find someone else's mouth to fill." My low voice quivered with desire.

A dark chuckle reverberated through his

chest. "But where's the fun in an easy target?" His words rumbled quietly as he backed away from me.

I stood there, still pressed against the low shelf for support, unsure of what to do. His words lingered in my mind and I'd hoped no other student had heard our exchange. I worked up the courage to head back to my desk and was met with a knowing look from Hawke. I did my best to ignore him and Colton for the rest of class as I set about organizing my assignment.

The class ran into the first break, and as I packed up my things, Eli came to talk to me. He looked genuinely concerned as he sat backward in the chair in front of my desk to face me. I must have been distracted the whole class as I didn't notice Frankie was absent. I was just glad Colton left me alone for the remainder of the lesson. His dumb comment had had its desired effect.

"You, okay?" Eli picked up one of my pens and twirled it in his long fingers.

"Yep, sure am." I grinned back at him and hoped it seemed believable. I didn't feel like discussing feelings.

"What are you doing this weekend?" he asked nonchalantly.

I paused and glanced at him. He sat there confident as fuck. "Nothing yet." I shrugged.

"Want to go catch a movie?" He handed me back my pen and gripped it tightly as I tried to take it from him. A mischievous grin danced across his face, and he knew what he was doing. He knew the effect he had on women.

"Miss Murdoch, a word. Now." Colton's voice broke the spell Eli had over me a moment before.

I heard Eli sigh as he stood. "I'll see you at lunch." His eyes darted to the teacher's desk before he left the classroom.

I grabbed my bag and made my way to Colton's desk. "Yes?"

"I won't have you flirting in my classroom. Organize your hookups outside of class. Now, get out." He tested me and I stood there, mouth agape.

"What's your problem?" I placed both my palms on his desk and leaned down so I was at eye level with him.

He ignored me and proceeded to write out a detention slip. He held it out to me with the cockiest smirk plastered on his perfect fucking face. I wanted to hit him. I wanted to scrunch up the detention slip and throw it in his face. There must be laws about teacher's being this mean to students for no reason at all.

"See you this afternoon, asshole." I snatched the slip from him and stormed out of the classroom.

I met up with Capri and her friends for first lunch. Eli was MIA, and I was secretly glad. I didn't want to tell him I got detention because of him asking me out on a date. As I sat sipping my coffee, I noticed Maddie stride in with her posse on her heels. Yes, this elite school served freshly made barista coffee with little school emblems decorated in cocoa powder on the froth. It was the one thing I did love about this place. One thing I didn't love was the queen bee, Maddie.

Her gaze fixated on me, and I sat up taller to let her know I wasn't afraid of her or her idiot friends. She narrowed her eyes as she pushed to the front of the line to pick up her lunch order. Fucking spoilt rich kids and their presumptuous tendencies.

"Peyton," Capri called out to me.

I slid my eyes to her. "Huh?"

Just as Capri was about to tell me something, the three assholes stormed through the dining hall in a flurry of determined haste. They pushed other students aside as they made their way to the exit and disappeared.

"Fuck." Capri reached across the table, grabbed my hand, and dragged me out of my seat to pull me through the dining hall after the three guys.

"Where are we going?" I allowed myself to be dragged along.

Capri didn't answer me; she was focused on not losing the guys as she led me through the maze of back passages through the school buildings. We exited through a fire escape to a part of the school I hadn't seen yet. From the looming canopy of the forest beyond the old stone fence, I worked out this was the very back of the school.

"After the guys." She dragged me through the dense forest until we broke free in a clearing with the high cliffs just beyond.

The roar of the angry ocean drowned out the thudding of my heart as I spotted the three guys staring over the edge. I knew something was wrong from the set of their shoulders; all three were dead still with their hands in their pockets. The only movement was the lapels of their jackets caught in the fierce wind.

"What are they doing?" I whispered to Capri, who had halted her steps and held me in place.

As though Steele heard me over the crashing waves, he turned to glare at me, his face masked in what I could only describe as satisfaction. His messy hair whipped his face as blasts of wind circled the clearing. I could see his narrowed eyes set firm in their resolve, and his mouth cocked up at the side in a poisonous sneer.

"Come on." Capri gripped my hand in hers like she was anchoring herself to me to stop them from doing something sinister, as we marched toward them. "Who is it?" Capri's voice came out in a shrill.

My stomach lurched. *Who is it?* What did she mean who is it? Was there a dead body down there? My mind raced with the possibilities that *they* had caught wind of my mom and I and were teetered on the edges of our lives again. Only *they* managed to pile bodies up as one would collect coins as a hobby. Only *they* disregarded human life like one discarded garbage.

I wanted to run back to the parking lot, jump into the car, and drive the fuck away from this town.

Steele's eyes slid to Capri, but his face remained the same. "Cameron Fletcher."

I felt Tyler's eyes snake across my skin; they pressed into me like a sharp sting. I swallowed and tried not to look up at him, but I couldn't stop myself. The guy I punched at the bonfire was dead at the base of the cliffs. I finally worked up the courage to look at Tyler, and his wicked smile knocked the wind out of me. Why the fuck would he be grinning about a dead student? Memories of him choking Cameron at the bonfire night sunk to the pit of my stomach.

I felt a sudden urge to hurl. It dawned on me then; the authority these kings had to do as they pleased, where no one would question them, was blaringly obvious. These fuckers would get away with murder.

"What the fuck did you do?" I blurted out,

and all eyes snapped to me. I felt Capri's hand squeeze mine, and I gripped hers back. I wasn't going to stand here and be scared of these ruthless fuckers.

"What's the matter, Bambi? You look caught in headlights again," Hawke mused as his gaze slammed into mine, not bothered by his dark curls blowing in his eyes in the harsh wind. Standing with his broad shoulders relaxed, he didn't look too concerned with what was going on.

"Better you two run along and pretend like you were never here." Steele's voice cut through the howl of the wind in a harsh tone as he flashed his pearly whites at me.

My eyes were drawn to the card in Steele's grip. The same card as I had found in my locker on my first day, only with gold font embossed into it instead of pink.

"Has it started again?' Capri's voice quivered, and I stole a side glance at her. Her eyes were glued to the card too.

I heard Steele whistle through pursed lips before he placed his hands behind his neck and looked up at the sky for answers. "We found it in Cameron's locker." His gaze returned to mine as he placed the card in his inner jacket pocket. The same place he had placed mine days earlier.

We stood in silence for a few seconds before we heard the soft thud of footsteps approach from behind us.

"Go back to class." Colton's voice broke the quiet. He genuinely looked concerned for his sister but when his eyes landed on me, his features changed. Gone was the concerned brother façade, it was replaced by something more quizzical.

"I'm not a kid anymore," Capri argued back.

"I'm not asking as your brother. This has nothing to do with you. Go before anyone catches you here. And don't fucking speak a word of this to anyone." He pressed his lips together in a hard line and turned to walk towards the cliff edge.

"Fuck my life," Capri huffed and stormed off toward the forest.

I stayed put and watched the guys discuss something in hushed tones. Their disregard for the dead student baffled me. Shouldn't they call the cops or the headmaster at least?

"Get the fuck out of here, Murdoch."

Colton's voice caught in a gust of wind and vibrated through me. His broad shoulders matched Steele's as they all huddled together. I realized they were all so much taller than the other male's at the school, and they were the only ones with visible tattoos.

I watched the four of them file one by one over the edge, down concealed steps, until they disappeared entirely. I crept forward and peered over the edge to see them standing around the dead body of Cameron, still in his St. Ivy uniform, sprawled on the wet sand. My gaze was transfixed on the body, and I was unable to move until I felt Tyler's gaze on me. He knew I thought he had something to do with this after the other night, and now they all had another reason to hate me even more.

There was no mention of Cameron for the rest of the day. Everyone was oblivious, and it didn't sit right with me. I wanted to tell the headmaster, but Capri begged me not to speak a word of it. I didn't know why, but she was convinced it had been dealt with already.

CHAPTER SEVEN

Peyton

I waited in his classroom for him. I waited like a good little schoolgirl, ready for my punishment. But he never showed. My fucking asshole stepbrother didn't even bother to show his face to dish out his stupid superiority and watch me suffer whatever torture he wanted to inflict on me.

My annoyance brewed within me as the time ticked on. I glanced around the classroom and spotted a box of chalk. Yep, this school was old school and still had the original blackboards in every classroom. I jumped off the desk and pushed the whiteboards covering the blackboard aside and set about my petty revenge. Once my beautiful artwork was done, I slid the whiteboards back across, grabbed my backpack, and left.

As I made my way across campus, I had a little pep to my step, and I couldn't wait for Colton to find the artwork I drew just for him. It was worth every detention until the end of the school year. The cartoon caricature of a giant dick with matching tattoos as Colton's, nearly took up the whole board. It was perfection personified and I mentally patted myself on the back.

I found myself in the foyer of the sports hall. I perused the sign-up forms for all the extra-curricular activities and found a few spots left for volleyball. Perfect. At my old school, I was on the senior girls' A team, and we won across the board, so you could say I wasn't terrible at the sport, and this would give me extra points for my college application.

As I pushed through the doors, my phone buzzed, and I glanced at the screen.

Capri: *Need a lift?*

Me: *Thanks, but I think I want to walk.*

Capri: *That's one long-ass walk!!*

Me: *I know, but I need it.*

Capri: *Love you, babe. Text me if you need me to come to get you.*

Me: *love you xx*

I sighed as I placed my phone back in my blazer pocket. Sometimes that girl knew me better than I knew myself. I hadn't told Capri all the sordid and dirty details of my past; I didn't think anyone needed to be burdened by that tale. I did, however, tell her some of it, and she broke down and cried and then apologized. Ever since then, she has been like a second mother to me, and although it's sweet and all that, I don't need anyone's pity.

I pulled out my coconut lip balm and smothered my lips before I headed out of the school gates and towards the beach. The sun was lower in the sky, and the start of a sunset kaleidoscope showed on the horizon. I loved this time of day, the colors, the smells, the lack of people around. I smiled at that last thought before I stopped and dropped my backpack to the ground. I pulled off my blazer and shoved it in my bag and decided to take my stupid school shoes off and shove them in too, along with the dumb knee-high socks we had to wear. I pulled my shirt out of my skirt and let it loose around my hips and instantly breathed a sigh of relief. I felt free somehow. Like the grips of the prestigious school weren't suffocating me anymore.

I hauled my backpack over my shoulders and set off down the beach. The wind carried with it the smells of salty air and sunscreen, the distinct scents of summer fading. The warmth of the sun tingled my skin, and I closed my eyes as I made my way to the water. It was cold and crisp as it lapped at my feet, and the coolness enticed me in further until the small waves were up to my knees, and thoughts of Steele that night at the party overtook my brain.

I waded through the shallow water towards home, past other mansions nestled along the shoreline, and nodded hello to the few people I saw along the way. Close to home, I spotted a lone surfer about one hundred yards from shore. I watched him as he floated out past the small breakers and wondered why he would bother on a day like today. The surf was nonexistent. He just sat there on his surfboard and watched the horizon as it darkened, his broad shoulders and back illuminated by the setting sun behind him.

I watched him for a good ten minutes as his body rose and fell with the movement of the ocean. I was so mesmerized by the movements I hadn't realized he'd turned to face the shore. He sat there and stared right back at me, no shame in his obvious gaze. I felt my skin heat at the thought of being caught ogling, but I didn't move. I couldn't physically move my legs to start walking. My shock when I realized it was Tyler out there pulled me out of my head and as I was about to walk away, I watched him slide off his board and dive under the water. He disappeared for a good long minute, my heart started to race, and I still couldn't make my legs move. For some reason, I needed to see him surface again.

The funny thing about the ocean and the distance to shore, you can't tell how far out a person is until they're closer to you than they were a minute ago. The sneaky bastard swam towards shore under the water, and I looked like an idiot just standing there as Tyler rose out of the waves like a mer god. His muscles shone like a golden beacon under the setting rays of the sun. I almost wiped my mouth to make sure I wasn't caught drooling.

He picked up his board and made his way toward me, a cocky grin plastered on his stunning face. The water beaded and dripped down his tanned muscles, and the golden glow of the sun highlighted the dips and planes of his abs, and my eyes drank him in and lingered on the number 5 tattooed between the deep V above the hem of his shorts. I allowed my eyes to take in every last bit of his skin before they snapped back up to his.

"Do you surf?" he asked, staring at me.

I swallowed whatever thoughts I'd had of him and managed to reply, "Nope."

"Ever tried?" He cocked his head to the side.

"Nope."

His smirk widened. "Can you say anything but nope?"

I shook my head. "Nope."

He chuckled. A melodic and masculine chuckle and ran his hand through his shiny black hair before he flicked the water at me.

"Hey!" I wiped my face.

"She speaks another word."

"You're funny," I replied sarcastically, glancing out at the ocean. I hadn't swum in so long, and the urge to strip down and run headfirst into the waves nearly overwhelmed me, but I remembered the reason why I'd not been semi-naked in front of anyone, and the thought put me in a sour mood.

"What are you doing out here this late and still in uniform?" His hungry eyes roamed my body before coming to a stop back on my face.

"Detention with my stepbrother." I scowled.

Tyler laughed and I couldn't help but think there was some secret joke I wasn't getting. "What did you do?"

"Fucking nothing." I crossed my arms.

"Colton doesn't dish the shit for no reason." Tyler narrowed his eyes at me as though he was trying to read my mind.

"I spoke to Eli after class, and Colton's a dick," I huffed and sounded like a typical, whiny teenage girl.

Tyler's tongue darted out and he licked his lip ring so fucking seductively, I nearly groaned. He looked as though he was about to say something when my phone buzzed. "Better get that." He raised his eyebrows.

I was confused at how normal and easy this conversation was and how it was so unlike any of our others. I shook that thought and pulled my phone out. It was Capri, and I quickly fired back a text to say I'll be home soon while Tyler stood and stared at me.

"I'll see you at school." He winked and strode up the sand towards the whitewashed mansion that sat pretty beyond the dunes.

I watched his muscles ripple over his back as he jogged up the beach before he disappeared into his yard, being swallowed whole like the sun into the horizon.

I stayed home for the entire weekend and got ahead on all my assignments and homework. I liked to be prepared for a disaster before it struck. I caught up on my favorite shows, put a conditioning treatment through my hair, and painted my toenails. By the time Sunday afternoon rolled around, I was relaxed and in a zone of bliss as my coconut-scented candle danced in the breeze and spread its sweet scent throughout my room. I hadn't run into Colton since I'd last seen him as he descended the cliffs. I hadn't heard another word about the poor dead kid, and I had pushed all thoughts of the three assholes out of my head. Eli never followed through on the movie date.

It was a good weekend.

Volleyball training was scheduled before school on Mondays. Who in their right mind scheduled shit for Mondays? I dragged myself out the door extra early as I was keen to walk to school, not that I'd admit to even myself that I hoped to run into Tyler along the beach again. The thought embarrassed me, and I wouldn't admit it to anyone, but the guy did things to my insides. He wasn't out surfing, and I couldn't help but stare at his house as I passed it in the hopes I might catch a glimpse of him.

I must have taken my sweet ass time to get to school because I was ten minutes late for training. The coach was understanding and said she'd bring me a uniform to change into and told me to go wait in the girls' changing rooms. I dumped my bag in an empty locker and closed myself into one of the cubicles because I was so fucking self-conscious of anyone seeing my scars. I waited for the coach to deliver the volleyball uniform and decided to strip off to not waste any more time.

I glanced at the back of the door and noticed there was no hook to hang my uniform on so I threw them over the door.

My fingers instinctively touched the scars on my hips. The raised scabs were like a roadmap to my inner demons. I glanced down and studied them, their faint redness slowly faded to match the other scars that marred my skin. Old scars that told a story of years gone. Stories of my torment and the hell I'd had to endure. I pulled the straps of my panties back over the scars when I heard a noise outside the cubicle. I froze and anticipated being caught, the adrenaline coursed through my veins as my heart beat in rapid succession against my chest. I felt like I needed to vomit. Being caught with my demons on full display made my anxiety peak. I felt the tingles as they started in my lips and spread towards my throat.

Breathe, Peyton. Count those fucking sheep.

My uniform disappeared over the other side of the door and to my horror, I heard thudded footsteps as the fucker escaped the girls' locker room.

"Fuck." I slammed my fist against the door in frustration. The impact of my punch made the whole row of cubicles vibrate and my knuckles instantly sting.

I'd have to wait for the coach to bring me my volleyball uniform before I could hunt down the guilty fucker. I waited and waited. There was no sign of the coach and no sign of my uniform returning. I didn't know how long I had waited there in nothing but my patent Mary Jane's, knee-high socks, and my Brazilian cut black lacy panties and bra. I always wore Brazilian cut panties; they hid the most skin at my sides. The skin where all my release was etched in perfect marks. I had to work up the courage to leave the cubicle now or risk it when the whole school would be filled with students before class. I knew I didn't have much time, but the logical part of my brain was overshadowed by the irrational part.

"Get your shit together," I gritted through clenched teeth. I glanced down at my sides and made sure to spread the hip part of my panties as wide as they would go. I took in a deep breath and stormed out of the door. There was not a soul in the changing rooms, and I had a sinking feeling this whole thing was a setup and not a quick opportunity. Either way, whoever the fuck did this was going to pay.

I strode to the lockers and yanked open the one where I had stashed my school bag earlier. Empty. Great. They now had all my possessions as well as my uniform. Well, they weren't going to take my dignity. I wasn't going to give them the satisfaction of seeing me affected by this juvenile shit. I was quite disappointed that this was all they could come up with. Pathetic.

I slammed the locker closed and spun on my heels. I spotted a clean hand towel neatly folded and placed next to the sink. Thank you, swanky elite school, for not using paper towels. I wrapped it around my ass and tucked the two corners into my panties. It would have to do until I found a teacher or someone to help me find something larger to hide behind.

My heart thrummed in my throat as I exited the girls' bathrooms and headed down the long hallway into the main stadium. I could hear faint voices echo through the hallway as my heart lurched in my chest, but I didn't stop walking, I strode right into the middle of the main stadium where half the senior class was gathered already.

I watched as they all slowly turned to face me, and nudged each other to get an eyeful of the new girl in nothing but her underwear. My glare zoned in on Maddie and her minions, a dirty smirk grazed her perfect face. A face I wanted pummel into the ground. Fuck her and her asshole friends. This wasn't going to break me. Nothing they could do would break me. I scanned the group for the culprit until my gaze landed on Steele, never too far from his little girlfriend. Typical teenage lovesick wankers.

He gave me a hungry once over and cocked an eyebrow as he nudged one of the other students with their back to him. Both Tyler and Hawke turned to stare, both just as surprised as the rest of the students. Good to know they probably had nothing to do with this from the looks on their faces. Steele on the other had probably put his little girlfriend up to it.

I wanted to crawl under a rock and

disappear, but I held my head high and strutted toward the faculty room in the hopes of finding a teacher to get me a spare uniform.

I could hear the snickers and whispers as I made my way to the faculty door. Someone cat-called me, and I wanted to shove a pen in their throat. I rolled my shoulders slightly and was well aware of the bounce of my tits. These babies were hard to hide when covered up, and now here they were, on display for all.

I stopped in my tracks as I entered through the door, Colton fucking Knight was in a heated conversation with the coach. His head turned slowly toward me, and his eyes practically bugged out of their sockets.

"What the fuck are you doing?" His tone sent shivers over my skin, even though he was always such an asshole.

"What the fuck does it look like?" I spread my arms for him to get a better look.

He headed straight for me, the rush of air as it left his lips, splitting the atmosphere. His tall frame came to a stop inches from my bare skin and sent turbulent desires, ones I tried to ignore, all the way down south. He smelled so fucking good, and I used all my self-control not to let out a quiet moan.

He gripped my elbow in his strong fingers as his dark gaze dripped with possession and ruin. "My office, now!" The silky smooth drawl of his voice did nothing to hide the undertones of his rage.

I had no time to argue as he pulled me through the room and out the back exit into a dimly lit hallway. In a split second he turned on me, his eyes wild with hateful lust, and his lips were pressed in a hard line. He let go and I felt the pulse of my heartbeat where the lingering pressure of his fingers remained.

Not even having made it to his office yet, he stopped and shrugged out of his leather jacket. "Put this fucking on." He pushed it into my chest, his fingers grazing over my breast as I was forced to grab the jacket.

"I'm fine. I just need my uniform." I shoved it back at him. I didn't need shit from him.

I heard the low rumble in his chest before his hands gripped my upper arms, he charged at me, and slammed his body against mine until I was sandwiched between him and the cold wall. My head flung backwards, the thud sent shock waves through me. I couldn't move.

I could barely breathe as his intoxicating scent circled through my senses. His hands moved and he pressed them against the wall on either side of my head The rough material of his jeans pushed against my skin and made heat rush to my core.

I glared up at him, and he glared back until his hot gaze slid to my throat. He didn't ease up on his pressure, and his eyes grew darker the harder he pushed into me. He adjusted his body slightly when his right hand came down and gripped my throat.

He studied me for a moment before he bared his teeth, hissed, and crashed his lips against mine.

My mind was a tornado of confusion mixed with need. My hand gripped the side of his shirt as his hard and punishing lips worked their magic on fueling my recklessness. I met his rage with my own and pulled him harder into me.

He yanked away. "Fuck." He groaned, almost in pain, and punched the wall next to my head. His breaths heaved in his chest, and he threw daggers at me like this was my fault.

I clenched my hand around his leather

jacket I still had in my grip. I was ready to mouth off when he threw his keys at me. Luckily my reflexes were quick or else they would have hit me in the face.

There was no casualness to his stance as he bared his teeth again. "Take my car and go get some fucking clothes on." He turned on the spot, stormed back through the door we came out of, and slammed it behind him. The scent of his masculinity hung in the air and the wrath of his rage torched my skin.

CHAPTER EIGHT

Peyton

I made it home and back to school in record time but decided to hang out in the library until first class was over. I handed in his keys at the office and told reception I had found them in the parking lot. There was no way I was going to sit through his class and have him punish me for what we did earlier. That was as much his fault as it was mine. I knew I'd fucking regret it later when I had to face him again. What the hell was I meant to tell Capri?

I ventured to the library. It had become my

favorite place to visit. It was always quiet and there was an abundance of books to choose from. Some dating back to the 1700s. I nodded to the librarian behind the desk and made my way to the third floor where all the old books were kept. I grabbed the first book I touched and settled down in one of the aged chesterfields. I needed to find my bag and uniform or I'd have to explain to my mom what happened and I didn't need her to worry about me.

Not long into the chapter, I heard muffled noises, and it piqued my interest. I stopped reading and waited. The sound of a low groan rang in my ears. I slowly got up and made my way along the wooden shelves, which were stacked to the brim with tomes, until I reached the end of the row. I peeked around and heard a dull thud and the sound of something drop to the floor. I crept further along the next bookshelf until I could see movement a few rows over. I could just barely make out the figures of two students through the gaps in the books. I snuck along until I was just out of sight and watched as one student grabbed the hand of the guy on the floor and twisted it. The distinct sound of a broken bone slipped through the air, sending a shudder through me.

I knew that sound all too well. My heart lurched in my throat at memories of those fucking bastards breaking my bones but never succeeding in breaking me. My fingers brushed over my left arm. Although the bone had healed, there was still a dull ache where his hands had landed. It was the last bone he had crushed and the last time I had the pleasure of smiling up at him while he tried to torture me. It always pissed him off that he could never get me to writhe in agony. He was always so hell-bent on trying to make me shed tears. It fed his fury.

The low groan of the student on the ground brought me back from my thoughts. I moved to get a better look when I realized the one doing the bone breaking was Hawke. His face was camouflaged with determination and calmness. Not the expression one would expect from someone inflicting pain on another. I watched him in fascination as he broke every finger on the guy's hand and then like it was nothing, dropped it, and studied the gagged student as he writhed in pain. Hawke moved then, enough to give the one holding the guy on the floor a direct view of me.

When he looked up, his eyes collided with mine, and a wicked smirk broke out across his face. Tyler stared at me as he held the student by the shoulders and winked like this was some sort of fun pastime they participated in regularly. I didn't move to hide; I just watched on as Hawke pulled the guy's leg up in his muscled arms and stomped on it. The crunch of bone echoed through me and I felt the throb of my heartbeat in my ears.

I stormed forward and pushed Hawke in the back. He stumbled over the guy's legs and into the row of bookshelves but managed to stop himself from falling over. He turned and lunged for me, only to be stopped by Tyler.

Hawke glared at me, his dark eyes filled with rage not seeing me at first. His hands gripped Tyler's as he came back from wherever he disappeared to a moment ago. Red rimmed dark eyes stared back at me as his fury slowly dissipated. I didn't back down and I sure as hell wasn't about to take any bullshit from him.

"You shouldn't be here," he gritted through clenched teeth as Tyler slowly let go of him.

"What the fuck did he do to you?" I pointed at the guy on the ground, his white shirt covered in bloodstains. Only, neither Tyler nor Hawke had any visible injuries.

"This is none of your business, Bambi. Leave." Hawke stepped closer to me and stared me down, his chocolate brown hair was a mess of curls atop his head and his eyes grew darker as they tested me.

My eyes flitted to Tyler as he stood back and kicked the guy on the ground to shut him up. His gurgled groans cut off immediately and the only sound was the air sucked in through his nostrils.

I raised an eyebrow. "I think it is my business if you're pulverizing another student."

"You don't know what you're talking about, sweetheart. You have no fucking idea what goes on in this place, and if you're smart, you'll stay the fuck out of it. Even better, leave the fucking school for good." Hawke nudged me with his rock-hard stomach, and I was forced to move back, his broad shoulders and extra height making me seem small in the moment.

I braced myself. Leaning forward into him, we were stomach to chest, pressed firmly into one another. Both stubborn and both not willing to back down. I watched his features as they morphed slowly back into the Hawke that roamed the halls. Gone was the haunted look of sheer hatred and what replaced it was something that confused me. Hawke tested my patience when he grabbed my hand in his and squeezed it. Not hard enough to break bones, but just enough to heed a warning.

"All right, you two." Tyler grabbed the back of Hawke's shirt and pulled him away from me.

I kept my eyes firmly plastered to Hawke's as he was dragged backwards. Something was hidden behind his casual façade, something fractured and slightly unhinged. A secret he so desperately wanted to keep to himself. He winked at me, but then his demeanor changed, and he turned to squat next to the injured student who was visibly in a lot of pain.

"You should go," Tyler whispered as his eyes snaked over me. "Stay out of this, Peyton." He leered at me, his voice had turned deadly serious.

It was the first time he had used my name since I'd arrived here, and the sound of it from his lips did unspeakable things to me. I really was fucking broken. Here I was being turned on by one of these guys while they beat the shit out of another student.

"Did you all have something to do with Cameron's death?" I blurted out without thinking.

"Get rid of her." Steele's voice snaked its way down my spine.

I knew he was right behind me. I could feel the warmth of his breath on the back of my neck. The male scent of him enveloped me as he brushed past my arm. I watched him in his school uniform and thought how deceiving it was. He wasn't a schoolboy. He was far from it. They all were. From the recent events, I concluded that these guys were ruthless and harbored no signs of remorse.

Not wanting to test them further, I turned on my heels and got the fuck out of there before I was witness to more of their torment. I escaped the library and headed to the square, where students rushed to get to their next classes.

"Peyton," Frankie called across the square.

"Hey." I headed straight for her. "Where have you been hiding?" I smiled.

"Don't even ask." She gripped my arm in hers and headed for the break in the square.

I tried to pry my arm from hers. "I have to get to class, I already missed this morning."

"I know. It's all through the school. Someone took photos and videos and posted them on their Instagram stories. Tiktok removed it already, though." She glanced at me with sympathy.

"Fucking awesome." I sighed.

We trudged through the forest and headed for the Club House, of all places. I was grateful as I didn't want to face the rest of the school yet, not that I had any shame of my body. But I didn't need everyone to have seen it.

"Don't worry about it. This whole thing will blow over by tomorrow. Someone else will be the talk of the school, and your delicious tits will be long forgotten." Frankie winked back at me as she held up her skull to unlock the door.

I burst out laughing. "Get in there." I shoved her through the door and closed it behind us.

The place smelled of faint remnants of cigar smoke and expensive whiskey. The scent brought back memories of those dark and long nights where the thought of dying was a welcome solution. Where the tight gag and the blindfold dug into my flesh and it always left marks. Where the blinding light, once it was all over, always made me think I had died and was on my way to the pearly gates.

Frankie touched my arm, and I jumped. "Want a drink?"

"Lemonade, please." I stalked over to the mantel above the fireplace and explored the photos on display. Some were in black and white and some in color. The only thing they all had in common was the ring on their finger. All the men in the photos wore the same skull ring as Colton and the three assholes.

"Here." Frankie handed me my glass with a slice of lemon and an umbrella on the side. "Figured you could use some sunshine and cheering up." She grinned and sipped her drink.

"It's working." I nodded and smiled at her gesture, the tightness in my chest lessened minutely "Who are all these men?" I quizzed.

She took a long swig before answering. "The founding fathers of Boat Harbor and the school."

"Why do you all have skull rings and pendants?" I had just turned to face her when the door creaked open.

"Found something that belongs to you." Tyler entered, holding up my school bag and uniform.

I narrowed my eyes at him and didn't move. A few moments ago, he was the accomplice in breaking bones and beating a student to a pulp, and now he was my savior again. Or was he?

"Don't you want your belongings?" he mused as he placed them on the long bar.

I crossed my arms and stared at him accusingly. "Where did you find them?"

"Swear to god, I didn't steal your shit and make you walk through gym half-naked. Although, I am very fucking appreciative of whoever did." He signed a cross over his chest and smirked like a deviant.

"Just shut up." I strode over to my bag and uniform, then pulled it off the bar and placed it by the stools, away from him.

"Want a drink, Ty?" Frankie chimed in, breaking the tension, heading around him to grab him a drink.

"Thanks, but some of us have class to attend." He winked at me before disappearing back out the door.

I stared at the door for a few moments trying to work him out. "Just before you found me in the square, Tyler and Hawke were in the library beating the shit out of some poor student." I turned to look at Frankie, who stared back at me.

"Don't read too much into it. This is what these boys do; they're full of testosterone and you know." She shrugged me off.

"No, I can't just ignore it. It's so fucking wrong." I threw back my lemonade and placed the cup in the sink behind the bar.

"Babe, there's nothing we can do. It's been the same since the beginning of this place. Rules are rules, and tradition is tradition. Neither of us can change it."

"And your mom is happy to turn a blind eye?" I raised my eyebrows.

"Hey, she doesn't turn a blind eye when it's not warranted," Frankie snapped back at me.

"Sorry." I shook my head to clear my thoughts. "I shouldn't have accused your mom of that. I'm sure she is handling things from her end." I gripped Frankie around the shoulders and squeezed her into me.

"I know it looks bad from the outside, but believe me, she is doing all she can." Frankie wrapped her arm around my waist and squeezed me back.

"You never answered me about the skulls," I probed further.

"They're just a silly gimmick that has been passed through the generations," she answered, and I knew to leave it at that. She wasn't going to elaborate any further.

"I guess I'd better get back to class." I walked back around to the barstools, picked up my uniform, and pulled my phone out of my blazer from this morning. Then I placed it in the blazer pocket I was currently wearing.

"You can hang out here with me until school ends," Frankie suggested, grinning.

"As tempting as that sounds, I need to face these fuckers head-on and deal with my photo being seen by all." I rolled my eyes and groaned.

"Go get 'em, tiger." Frankie winked as she passed me and settled on one of the chesterfields.

I giggled and shook my head at her. "Do you ever go to class?"

"Not if I don't have to. If you're ever looking for me, I'll probably be here." She smiled as she sipped her freshly made drink.

"Wish me luck." I threw my bag over my shoulder and headed for the door.

"You won't need it, babe, but good luck anyway." She blew me a kiss before I exited and made my way back to the square.

My phone buzzed in my jacket pocket, and I pulled it out to stare at the screen.

Almost instantly, my throat felt like it was about to close up as panic tingled through my veins. My eyes darted around the square and searched each dark corner and every last hiding place for him. How the fuck did he get my number? I looked back at my phone and swiped the text message.

Dylan: *How's Boat Harbor treating you? You left without saying goodbye.*

The ache in my heart was instant, closely followed by the horror realization. Fuck. I had

116

to keep this from my mom. If she knew someone from back there had found us, she'd have us packed up and shipped out of here in an instant. I swallowed my dread as I tried to think of a good response.

Me: *Hey! You know how my mom is. Please don't tell anyone you know where I am. Miss you.*

I hit send and waited for his reply.

Nothing.

The rest of school went by in a blur of snickers, whispers, and straight-out propositions. Even after I punched one dick in the face, the taunts didn't stop. By the end of last class, even Capri had had enough and was telling everyone to fuck off. I was never going to live this down. I was probably going to be forever known as the new girl who strutted through the gym half-naked. Even Eli avoided me the entire day. I spotted him at first break, but he did an about-turn and stormed away in the opposite direction.

Just when I thought things couldn't get worse, Dylan texted me back.

Dylan: *Waiting in the parking lot.*

CHAPTER NINE

Peyton

There he stood beside his sleek red Ducati in ripped jeans, a faded black t-shirt, and riding boots. He looked more muscled than I remembered and he had a hell of a lot more tattoos over his tanned skin. I watched as the other students stared when they passed him, but their scrutiny and upturned noses didn't faze him. Not much *did* phase Dylan; he was oblivious to the outside world, and only those close to him mattered.

"A friend of yours?" Capri nudged me.

"You could say that." I swallowed my nerves,

though I had no fucking idea why I felt nervous. This was Dylan, my Dylan. The one who picked up my pieces and placed them all back together as best he could.

"Hell, he looks like more than a friend the way his possessive ass is staring at you." Capri snickered. "I'll wait at my car if you need me." She gripped my hand, leaned up, and kissed me on the cheek.

"Love you." I kissed her cheek in return.

"Love you." She sauntered off to her car, never taking her sights off Dylan.

I took a deep breath and skipped down the steps toward him. His grin grew wider the closer I got until I was just out of reach. Before I could say anything, he lurched forward wrapped his arms around my waist, and lifted me up for a big bear hug.

My arms instinctively circled his neck, and I squeezed him as though my life depended on it. It felt so good to be in his protective arms again. He felt safe and like home. Something I hadn't realized he made me feel until this very moment.

He placed me back on the ground and let go of me. His eyes sparkled with adoration and guilt. "Look at you, miss preppy." He reached out and took a strand of my hair in his fingertips. "What's with the white hair?"

"Don't." I play punched him in the arm and he let go of my hair, tucking it behind my ear instead.

"I fucking missed you," he confessed.

"I fucking missed you too." It was true. I'd missed him terribly, even though he was mixed up in my tormented past.

His eyes scanned the looming school buildings behind me, a small smirk upturned the corner of his mouth. "So, this is your new school, huh?" His narrowed gaze returned to mine.

I shrugged. "Yep." I couldn't work out why he was looking at me the way he was. "What's with all the muscles and tattoos?"

He raised a brow. "You noticed?"

"Bit hard not to. Look at you." I teased.

He spun on the spot to give me a full view of his back and then turned back to face me. "You like?" He winked.

"You haven't changed." I laughed at him.

"You didn't answer my question." His eyes darkened slightly, and this unnerved me.

"You know I like everything about you. You're my knight in shining armor." I held my breath at the thought of all the times he saved me from myself and those monsters.

His gaze froze on something to my right, and he cocked his head slightly. I felt the hostility as it radiated from him, and his nostrils flared. I turned to see what had put him in a sudden mood only to spot the assholes descending the stairs while Colton trailed behind them.

My present collided with my past in that instant as Colton, Steele, Tyler, and Hawke all exited through the ornate school gates and halted their steps when they spotted me here with Dylan. I looked up at him, but his eyes were focused on the four, almost as though recognition etched his features.

He broke his stare and looked back down at me. "I'm going to go, but you have my number now. Use it." He pulled me in for another death grip, this hug more possessive than friendly.

"I will," I said, breathlessly as he let go of me.

"I'll come back another time." His gaze flitted to the St. Ivy gates before he climbed on his motorbike, revved the engine, and took off like a maniac out of the school grounds.

I watched the road where he disappeared as confusion rocked my insides. Why did he show up to only leave after a few minutes? I didn't get it. Did he know those assholes and Colton? I'd have to pull Tyler aside and pick his brains about Dylan, since he was the one who seemed the least pissed off and hateful with me. My mind ran a thousand miles a minute at all the scenarios of why he was here and why he had tracked me down. I had no unfinished business back there, and there was nothing but a close friendship between us. He knew all my dark secrets and all my pain and misery. He was there afterward, consoling me and tending my wounds. He was the one who took me to ER and ensured I had the best treatment, all secretly and untraceable to the ones who had tortured me.

I'd have to keep this from my mom. She couldn't know he was here in Boat Harbor. I didn't think she would survive any more shit from our past. Her guilt and heartache chipped away at her mental state ever since she worked out what the fuck was going on when she was out of town for business trips.

It eats at her every damn day, even though none of this was her fault. None of what happened to me had anything to do with her.

The four of them sidled up beside me while I was still staring at the road, lost in my thoughts.

"Stay the fuck away from him, Peyton." Colton's voice came out all harsh and deadly.

I turned to face him only to find all four of them towered over me. "What the fuck is your problem?" I glared at him.

Colton's jaw tensed. "Him." His eyes darkened a shade, their piercing ocean green turning to a shade of nightfall.

"You're fucking pissing me off right about now." My hands flexed into fists at my side.

"Your fuck buddy is lucky I don't fucking skin him alive. Make sure he stays out of our town, or he'll lose more than just the most important thing to him." His eyes were trained on me, and I got the impression that when any of them spoke, they meant something entirely different.

I stepped away from them, as I needed the distance. I didn't deny the accusation of Dylan being my fuck buddy and I wanted Colton to stew in his own stupidity.

My gaze connected to each one of theirs. The other three stood silent and let Colton do all the talking. Like he was their pack leader. It was pathetic. "Whatever." I huffed, stepped around them, and headed to Capri's car. I fully expected one of them, mostly Steele, to jut out an arm to stop me. But they didn't; they let me leave in peace. No smart-ass comments, no throat grabs, no broken bones, and most importantly, not another mention of Dylan.

I climbed into Capri's car, and she looked at me like I'd kept the biggest secret from her. *If she only knew the whole truth.* "Don't look at me like that." I pulled my seatbelt on and sunk back into the seat.

"Who the fuck was that hot piece of ass?" She pretended to wipe up drool.

"A friend from my past. No one, really. I don't even know why he showed up." I watched the passing ocean as we drove home.

"Oh, honey, I know exactly why he showed up." Capri turned the volume up on her favorite song.

I left that statement to linger in silence for a long while as I kept my eyes on the ocean.

Finally, I turned to look at Capri just as we neared home. "It's not like that." *It's far from that,* I thought to myself. No one would want to touch me after seeing me go through the shit I went through. No one with half a brain and no one with a heart as big as Dylan's.

Capri gripped my hand in hers and held it firm. "Are you okay? After this morning?"

"I'm okay. It would take a lot more than that to crush me." I kept my eyes on the ocean.

"The pic was taken down from Instagram, if it makes you feel any better." Capri turned into the driveway and parked the car in the garage.

I simply smiled at her and got out of the car.

I walked straight to my room and dumped my bag beside my bed before heading for the bathroom. I turned the hot water on to fill the oversized lavish bath, then dropped in a galactic bath bomb. I watched it fizz and hiss as it bobbed and swirled around the bathtub, the scent of cotton candy soon filling the bathroom. I grabbed all my favorite candles and placed them on the window ledge overlooking the ocean and lit them. The coconut smell mixed with cotton candy took me to a place of magical dreams.

My therapist once told me that scents could transport you to different memories. That was probably why I had a hard time smelling cigars and expensive whiskey. It dredged up the smells of those nights where I was passed around from one to the next, all to pay a life debt thanks to my fuckwit father, who couldn't keep his head on when playing with one of Dev's best girls and ended up killing her. Only to offer me up in her place.

Coconut on the other hand made me think of the beach and summer and days spent on holidays, and at that minute it was where I wanted my mind to go, so I stripped off and climbed in to soak my worries away. I barely even got to the pruning stage when Capri barged in and held up a giant gold dildo.

"Holy fucking shit! Holy fucking shit!" She paced across my bathroom without caring that I was in the bath. I stared at her shocked and bemused.

"Why are you swinging that thing around in here?" I asked, and tried not to laugh as I covered my tits so she couldn't get an eyeful.

"This! This here is the invitation of all invitations." She kept pacing.

"I'm guessing you're excited then?" I chuckled and sunk further into the bathwater. The bath bomb had turned the water a pretty purple color, and I hoped it didn't tinge my hair ends.

Capri stopped and sat on the edge of the bath, holding the dildo right in front of my face for me to read.

"Okay, it has writing on it." I looked at her, unsure of what I was supposed to be excited about.

She exhaled and clutched the dildo to her chest. "It's an invite to the most exclusive party of the year!"

"But why send it on a dildo?' I looked at her confused.

"Well, there are legends and myths about what goes on at these parties." She waggled her eyebrows at me.

"I'm happy you got an invitation." I smiled at her and cupped my tits tighter.

"Holy fuck, have you checked your bag?" She scrambled up and ran into the room.

"No, I haven't," I said quietly to myself. There was no point to shout it to her as she had probably already emptied the entire contents of it on my floor.

A high-pitched squeal rang in my ears, and I sprung out of the bath, almost tripped over the fluffy bathmat, and grabbed the towel to wrap around me. As I scurried to see what Capri squealed about, she rushed at me with another huge dildo in her hand. Only, this one was red. She waved them around excitedly like some dildo wielding samurai.

"You got an invite. You got an invite!" She grabbed my arms and started to jump up and down, making me join her in her excitement.

The door to my room flung open, and my mom rushed in to see me, naked with a towel on, and Capri jump around with two giant dildos.

"Should I come back?" Mom looked equally horrified and amused.

"Ahh, Nicki!" Capri launched herself at my mom and gripped her in a tight hug. The dildos flopped about my mom's head. A sight I never wanted to see again.

Once Capri stopped jumping around like a lunatic, Mom gripped her shoulders and made her breathe to slow her down. "What in the world are you two doing?" She giggled.

"It's not what it looks like, I swear. They're invites to some exclusive party or something," I explained while Mom helped Capri calm down, a small smile still curved the edge of her mouth. I wrapped the towel around me a little tighter and hoped it stayed in place.

"It's the party of parties. The one everyone wants to get invited to. You have no idea what this means," Capri said while gripping the dildos for dear life.

"Sounds exciting. When's this party? Do we need to go shopping?" Mom looked at me and shrugged. I was glad she was as clueless about this whole thing as I was.

Capri squinted as she read the small scrawl printed on the dildo. "Says tonight. Fuck!" She squealed and jumped up and down on the spot.

"What's the dress code?" Mom looked at me again.

"No idea?" I shrugged and headed back into the bathroom to pull the plug out of the bath. So much for a relaxing soak.

"It says on here to wear dark formal attire. Each recipient of a colored invite must wear that color to the party. Half skull face paint must be applied or no entry. A private driver will collect invitees and drop them off at a secret location where another private car will collect you and transport you to the secret location of the party. All phones and cameras are forbidden. Anyone caught with either, will be removed and punished. Enter at your own risk."

I screwed up my face. "Red is not my color."

"Oh, baby, you just need the right shade. I have both red and gold dresses if you girls want to borrow them. I'll call in my hairdresser and get her to bring a make-up artist. Let's start getting ready." Mom winked at me as Capri gripped her in a bear hug again.

"Thank you," I mouthed to my mom. She was so good for Capri, who had never met her mom, as she had passed away during childbirth.

"Go have a shower and be ready for hair and makeup in thirty." She stepped out of Capri's hug and tapped her on the ass to get her to start moving.

Capri threw the dildos on my bed and disappeared toward her room without another word, and Mom followed her out of the room to find the dresses for us. I threw open the doors to my balcony and stood against the railing to admire the ocean and let its calm ease my anxiety. My eyes caught sight of movement down near the pool. Colton stared up at me, his muscled chest and abs on spectacular display; he wore nothing but swim shorts. His eyes never left mine, as though he dared me to join him. His gaze sent fire through me and made my heart falter.

I glared back at him as sweat beaded over the nape of my neck, and images flashed behind my eyes. Images of him as he crashed his lips into mine. He broke the spell and dove into the pool, disappearing under the water.

CHAPTER TEN

Peyton

The sunset turned the sky on fire as Capri and I waited on the front porch for our driver. Both our faces were painted in matching half skulls. My mom had saved the day and prevented Capri from a meltdown.

I glanced down at my outfit, a deep red dress that clung to my curves and had two splits that went up to the tops of my thighs. The smooth satin material flared slightly from my hips and billowed out behind me when I walked. My entire back was exposed and the thin straps over my shoulders were all I had holding the gown up. I had paired the dress with my favorite jewel-encrusted Armani stilettos, and they sparkled in the afternoon glow. The hairdresser had loosely braided my long hair to the side with loose tendrils to frame my face. I felt like a fucking queen, and I was secretly glad to have been invited.

"I'm so fucking nervous." Capri gripped my hand.

"Why?" I didn't get why this girl had anything to be nervous about. She was the epitome of stunning. Her copper hair matched her gold dress perfectly. She looked like a goddess.

She glanced at me. "I don't know. What if we don't know anyone there?"

"We've got each other. We'll dance and drink and have fun." I squeezed her hand in reassurance.

Both our eyes flitted to the blacked-out Rolls Royce as it rolled to a stop in front of us. The driver climbed out, wearing tails and a gold skull mask made of metallic material. He didn't speak as he made his way to the back door and opened it before waiting for us to file in.

"Ready?" I grinned at Capri's skull-painted face.

She pulled me forward and dragged me into the car. "Fuck yes!"

After we sat inside and the door shut, I paled. "You do realize we can't see out of the windows, right?" A small panic started to edge its way into my belly.

"Oh." Capri twisted in her seat to look out the back window. It too was blacked out.

I leaned forward and tapped on the divider glass, getting no response just as the car started to move forward. "I guess we're stuck now." I shrugged and sat back in my seat.

"Here." Capri pushed herself into me to take a selfie. "We should at least have a few pics before our phones get confiscated." She kissed my cheek as she took a photo.

"I didn't even bring mine. There's nowhere to put it, I mean, I'm not even wearing any panties." I glanced down at my dress.

"Me either." Capri burst out in laughter. "This dress is so tight, even my panties that are supposed to be seamless still showed." She pressed her face against mine, making me take a few more photos and silly videos, then proceeded to post them on Tik Tok and Instagram.

I played with the hem of my dress. "Do you think anyone from school will be there?" My quiet anxiety slowly started to grow in the pit of my stomach. I just needed to hold it together tonight. My mom's words rang in my ears. *If you don't like it, you can always leave. No one will force you to do anything you don't want to ever again. Just leave, Peyton. Find a cab and come home.*

When I felt an attack brew, I always turned to decorating my skin. This felt like pure torture, being stuck in this car without a view outside. It felt like my entire being was blindfolded, not just my eyes. I could feel the pressure slowly build, needing an outlet. I did all I could to not try to claw my way out of the car. My veins burned and my lips tingled as the car drove on to our unknown destination. I needed to trust myself and my instincts and not bow to my fears.

"Hey." Capri gripped me around the neck. "I got you tonight, okay?" She pulled me into her. I was so grateful for this beautiful woman and how she sensed when I needed her.

"I know." I leaned on her shoulder as the car started to slow down thanks to the bumpy road and finally stopped at our next destination.

"If you want to go home, we can turn around and get the fuck out of here." Capri held my gaze as she tried to pry the truth from my lips.

I couldn't deny her, or me, some fun. I had to remind myself that this was an innocent party. High school kids dancing and getting drunk or high. Not an exclusive gentleman's club where they passed around women like platters of food, each taking what they wanted when they wanted without question or consequence.

"Let's go." I grinned at her and tried my best to turn my thoughts around.

Capri raised her eyebrows. "Are you sure?"

"I'm sure. Let's go have some fun. Fuck knows we need it." My eyes darted to the opened car door where the driver stood waiting.

"Okay." Capri nudged me out.

We climbed out into the middle of a forested area. The sun had long since set, and the cleared area was illuminated by a circle of lanterns, their flames dancing manically in the cool breeze. The lanterns extended down the long narrow driveway and disappeared around a bend. The entire place felt eerie and haunted with the looming canopy of the tall trees that surrounded us. The stars were already out and twinkled down on us like a speckled mess.

"This is a bit much." Capri whistled through pursed lips. "Like any of us would tell their little secret hideaway." She scoffed.

A group of girls was huddled in the center of the clearing, and I noticed they were dressed in gold dresses. I glanced down at what I wore and wondered if I was invited to the same party as the rest of these guests. "I'm the only one in red."

"That's weird. Maybe they transport us in different groups?" Capri shrugged.

Easy for her to be so blasé about it; she wasn't the one who stood out. "Maybe."

"Let's go mingle." Capri linked her arm through mine, and we joined the others near the center. I didn't recognize anyone, and it seemed that no one knew each other since they all stood separately.

The awkward silence was interrupted by the

noise of tires as they crunched on the gravel road and a convoy of blacked-out Bugatti's circled into the clearing and stopped around us. As if practiced to perfection, all the doors opened in a synchronized fashion, and a skull-masked driver exited each vehicle.

"Do we just go pick a car?" I asked Capri, who looked equally as confused as the rest of the girls near us.

"I guess." Capri shrugged but didn't budge.

One of the other girls stepped forward and made her way to the car at the front of the line and proceeded to climb in. She seemed to have an idea of what was going on so we all followed. I jumped in the car nearest to us, and Capri climbed in the car in front of mine. When all girls were safely seated, the drivers circled to the driver's side, climbed in, and revved their engines.

I had no fucking idea of where we were, but I was thankful to be able to see through the front windshield. I didn't think I could have handled another car ride where the windows were blacked out. I glanced at the driver in his gold mask and wondered what he thought about this whole setup. We sat in silence as he followed the cars in front through deserted streets. It felt like they deliberately weaved through the streets to disorientate us. The car cabin was a mask of darkness until the brake lights of the cars in front lit up and turned the golden mask the driver wore into something from a horror movie.

Each car stopped, and when it was my turn to get out, I opened my door and slid out before the driver could assist me. He offered his hand, but I didn't accept it. Instead, I stood and looked around. The street was deserted, blocked off by road barriers at each end, and a guard was posted to keep watch.

I glanced around as Capri made her way over to me. "Where are we?"

She shrugged. "I have no idea, but it looks like we're about to find out."

Our drivers each stepped up, effectively separating us, and started ushering us individually through the entrance of the building. Like we were being showcased or some bullshit. Each leading us up a thick carpet that paved the path from the cars to the front of the building.

Walking through the front double doors, I

couldn't help but admire the ostentatious building where red velvet couches and white pillar candles decorated the foyer. The walls were made of dark paneled wood, and the entire building gave off a moulin rouge crossed with a horror circus vibe. A skull-masked usher called us up to the desk and handed over a form for each of us to sign.

"Please read carefully and if you agree to these terms, sign at the bottom." He placed two pens down and proceeded to busy himself behind the desk.

I was about to read what I was signing when Capri nudged me. "Just sign it," she whispered.

I rolled my eyes at her and signed my life away. Too late to back out now. It was time to finally let my hair down and have some *fun* again.

The usher held up two wristbands and gestured for us to extend our wrists to have them put on. "Keep these on all night. If it gets torn off, damaged, or you lose it, it's immediate removal from the premises. You will not be permitted to re-enter. If you feel you need a break or need to leave, exits are located on the right side of the building on all levels. Once you're out, you're out. Anything you see, hear, or participate in is not to be repeated. Period. Place your phones and cameras in here." His eyes moved and landed on me as he placed a small safety deposit box on the desk.

Capri hesitated before she placed her phone in. I held up my hands to show I had nothing on me.

"Your phone will be returned to you." His gaze remained on me as he shut and locked the safety deposit box.

A shiver snaked its way down my spine as he stared at me and gave off serial killer vibes. Maybe it was the mask? Either way, I was happy to get the fuck away from him and enter the top-secret party.

"Welcome to hell, ladies." He said it like he was bored shitless already, and I felt his eyes on me as we stepped through the black velvet curtain.

CHAPTER ELEVEN

Peyton

Immediate sensory deprivation cloaked us as we made our way down a pitch-black hallway, with no light or sound from anywhere.

I reached out to grab Capri. "I can't see shit."

"I've got a hold of the wall, so I'll keep us straight. Just grab on to me," she replied, her voice strained.

"How fucking long is this passage?" My question was answered when I bumped into the back of Capri. "Shit, sorry."

"Can you feel around for a door handle or

something?" I felt Capri's arms wave around.

I couldn't help but giggle at this absurd situation.

"Shhh." Capri snorted as we both tried to feel around for anything to get us the hell out of the pitch-black narrow hallway.

A blinding light appeared to our left, and a passage was revealed as a door slid to the side. I squinted into the glare as a skull mask appeared and stared back at us. I could barely make out what was beyond the doorway as my eyes adjusted to the assault of the light.

"This way." He pointed to the brightly lit passage.

I grabbed Capri's hand and just as we both stepped into the new passageway, the door closed behind us with a final thud. I glanced back to see the masked guy stand and wait for the next poor person to get stuck in the dark. This hallway was pristine white with fluorescent lights that seemed to get brighter the further we ventured. I started to think this was a rabbit hole full of mazes that just circled, and we'd be forever stuck in perpetual blinding light or pitch black.

We stopped at the end where an exit sign shone above but there appeared to be no exit.

I turned around to see an empty hallway. The skull masked guy was gone. "This isn't funny anymore." I scowled.

Capri knocked on the wall with her closed fist. "Open the fucking door," she shouted and her voice echoed around us.

"At least we can see in here, even if we're half-blinded." I glanced over my dress and ran my palms over the silky-smooth material before I placed them on the wall in front of us. The wall seemed to vibrate under my fingertips in time to my heartbeat.

Capri pressed her ear against the wall and listened. "I think I can hear a faint something."

The wall clicked, and we both jumped back as it slid to the side, and a whoosh of thumping base pressed against my chest. The music emanating from this new room took my breath away. The sound of *Dark Side* by Bishop Briggs filled my senses as the darkened room before me slowly revealed itself.

"Wow." Capri gaped at the scene before us. She gripped my hand in hers and pulled me into what appeared to be an enormous private club.

Wow was one way to put it. The room lived

and breathed a hedonistic sexual tension, all the way from the dim lighting and the foggy smoke to the fire twirlers perched on platforms on either side of the room. I watched, mesmerized, as one swallowed the flames only to then spit fire into the air and spin around to relight her twirler.

"What the hell is this place?" I asked as we stepped further into the main club area and the door behind us shut. I spotted a girl high up in a metal birdcage dressed in a strappy bondage suit. She smoked a cigarette as she moved to the rhythm of the music. My eyes roamed the red-hued room and settled on the two naked performers on the stage. Their sensual dance captivated me as they bled over each other and moved their bodies in sync.

Capri glanced at me. "Is that real blood?"

"I doubt it." I couldn't avert my eyes as the female dancer straddled her partner and began to ride him. I admit it was fucking hot.

The place was already filled with skull-masked faces. All the men wore tails, and all the women were dressed in gold evening dresses. I glanced down at my dress; the moody lighting made it look as though I had a dress on that dripped blood.

Capri led me to the closest bar to order drinks. "I'll have a water, thanks," I told the barman, and Capri shook her head and stifled a laugh. "Someone needs to look after your drunk ass."

"I know." She giggled and ordered herself some fancy cocktail I'd never heard of.

My eyes scanned the room to maybe find another woman dressed in red. No such luck. I began to get the feeling that I had been singled out for a reason. I then spotted a staircase that led to the second floor. It was darker up there than down here, and I wondered what was up there that needed to be so hidden from plain sight.

"Let's go find a seat." Capri headed to the left of the bar, and past the main stage area, where the red velvet booths and aged chesterfield couches were scattered.

We sat and took it all in. I noticed the female servers were dressed in sexy lingerie with their faces painted in gold. The male servers were all dressed in tails, and the only thing that differentiated them from the male guests was that they wore golden skull masks and the guests had their faces painted as skulls. What was with the skulls theme?

The music changed into a dance rhythm, the bass vibrating through the floor and up the chair legs. I could feel it in my bones as it thumped repeatedly. I licked my lips and opened my bottle of water to take a sip when three sexy as hell guys sidled up to our booth. Their faces disguised behind painted skull masks, which made them all the more alluring. The one with smoothed back blond hair tilted his head as he studied me.

"Ladies." The one with dark hair grinned.

I knew that voice. It was Tyler, and I presumed the other two were Steele and Hawke.

"Great," I muttered under my breath. Not that anyone could hear their thoughts let alone their voice thanks to the volume of the music.

"Follow us." He glared at me, obviously expecting me to just jump up and do as he ordered.

"No thanks. We're good here," I challenged him.

Tyler leaned down and placed his palms on the table right in front of me. "I'm trying to do this the nice way. So, get up and come with us or this will get messy." He threw me a shit-eating grin.

"Let's just go. Fucking Colton has probably put them up to it." Capri rolled her eyes and let Tyler help her out of the booth.

I sighed and figured what choice did I have here? I could fight them on this and get dragged to where they wanted me, or I could go willingly and stay with Capri. I ignored Tyler's extended hand and climbed out of the booth myself. Then I followed after Hawke and Steele as they parted the crowd on the dancefloor, both heading to the stairs that led to the second floor. Did the air just get colder up here?

Capri glanced at me as we reached the top of the stairs, and her look of shock did not mirror my face. I had seen this and so much fucking worse. I grabbed her hand and gave it a reassuring squeeze as the two performers carried out their act on the plush king-sized bed. The naked woman was on her hands and knees as her partner pleasured her with a massive glow-in-the-dark vibrator. I could see the quiver of her thighs as her orgasm threatened to overtake her, and it brought back violent memories I had locked away in a deep vault inside my brain.

"Come on, let's get another drink." I pulled Capri away from the performers on the bed, and the three assholes, before dragging her back towards the bar. Steele, Tyler, and Hawke disappeared to sit on their thrones in the back corner of the room where a group of giggling girls joined them. I tried not to glance their way but failed. I had no place to feel the slight ebb of jealousy weave its way into my thoughts.

After Capri threw back a few shots that she said she needed to get through the show up here, I sent her to sit with some of the other women who had all huddled together. I sucked in a deep breath and leaned on the bar to get my head in the right place.

The air shifted around me, and I felt magic prickle my skin. Dark magic of black smoke and white fire heated my exposed back as he pressed against me. I knew his scent. I knew it was him, even if I couldn't distinguish him from the others. Dylan breathed on my neck, and his hot lips hovered over my skin. Sparks danced before my eyes. Everything in this place was amplified. My skin felt like it was on fire when he spoke.

"You're not safe, Blue," he whispered.

I hated it when he called me that, and he fucking knew it. I tore my gaze away from the show and turned to face my intruder. He took my breath away with his dark eyes emphasized by his painted skull mask. He stood over me, and a crease formed between his eyebrows.

"Don't call me that." I gripped the bar behind me.

He watched me intently, and a grin spread over his painted face. "Still a fighter, I see."

"I have nothing I need to fight here."

He leaned in; and his eyes focused on my mouth. "Are you sure?"

"Yes." I crossed my arms in front of me. I didn't want him getting any closer. He knew all my deep and dark secrets, and the last thing I needed was the others being alerted to him being here.

"Tell me then, your friends aren't hassling you, are they?" His gaze scanned the room and locked on the performance on the bed.

"Nothing I can't handle," I said in defense.

His top lip curled over his teeth, and his eyes dropped to my body. "I don't doubt it."

"What are you doing here? If the others-"

He held up his hand to halt me from

speaking. "The others can't do shit to me." His jaw tightens at that statement.

I narrowed my eyes. "What's that supposed to mean?"

"Things have changed, Blue. You'd be surprised."

I snorted. "Yeah, fucking right. That place is worse than the pits of hell. I don't know why you don't get out. You're too good for them." I blinked up at him. I always knew he was better than the rest of them. He had a pure heart when it came to the people he cared for, but he could just as easily turn his heart off and torture someone like the best of them.

"I need you to do something for me." He kept his gaze on me and lifted a hand to gently brush from my cheek down my neck to my shoulder. His touch was whisper light and hesitant, nothing like the confident Dylan I knew.

"I knew it. I knew you were here for a reason. What the hell do you need, Dylan?" I demanded, stiffening my shoulders and waited for the verbal blow to come.

He leaned down until his lips were against my ear. My heart thundered in my chest. I wasn't sure if it was from him being here in my new life or from the bass of the music.

"You need to come back for one night."

I pushed him away as my anger burrowed deep in my gut. "I don't fucking think so. Are you fucking crazy?"

"Hear me out." His voice was cut off as he was hauled back away from me.

I watched him spin on the spot and swing out to connect with the jaw of the guy who had a grip on his suit jacket. In a blur of movement, the three assholes descended and broke up the fight. I watched as Dylan was escorted out, the three assholes disappearing with him, and my heart ached a little for him. I knew this wasn't going to be the last time I laid eyes on him. I knew it in my gut that I'd be summoned back for one night. The matter, was whether I went willingly or not.

My eyes collided with Capri's; she stood a few feet away with a guy beside her. She waved at me, and I pushed off the bar and strode over to her.

"Was that your friend from today?" She wrapped her arm around my neck and pulled my face into hers.

I nodded. "It was."

Capri's eyes darted to Jasper and back at

me. "I can tell him to go away if you need to talk or something." She kissed my cheek.

I glanced over at him. He looked so good in his suit. "Hey." I grinned at him.

"You all good?" He nodded once.

"I am, thanks." I smiled gratefully, knowing at that moment that he was good enough for Capri.

"Let's go dance." Capri grabbed mine and Jasper's hand.

"Maybe later. I'm going to sit for a bit and watch the show." I waggled my eyebrows and watched Capri's face scrunch up.

"I'll leave you to it." Capri kissed me on the cheek again and dragged Jasper downstairs.

My veins tingled, and I couldn't sit still. The adrenaline still burned in me from before when Dylan revealed the real reason for coming to Boat Harbor. I didn't know what possessed him to even think I'd ever step foot back in that cesspit. I shook off the feeling of disgust and headed down the stairs for a better look at this place.

The dance floor was packed with bodies all pressed up against one another. It was hard to distinguish who was who when they were all dressed the same with nearly identical painted faces. The vision was disturbing. I slowly made my way past the couples fucking on every available surface until my gaze caught two guys aggressively sucking face. I stopped and watched them in fascination; they were so angry and possessive of each other that I couldn't look away. As if they sensed me watching them, they broke their kiss and turned to look directly at me. The one with the neck tattoos tilted his head and winked at me before he gave his masked friend another sultry kiss and strode off into the crowd.

The one that remained against the wall continued to stare at me and caused goosebumps to spread down my spine. It was then that I worked out it was Hawke and Tyler, and it sent turbulent desires to my core. Hawke's venomous glare rooted me to the spot. He looked pissed that I had interrupted them and before he could venture over to me, I escaped to the front to watch the stage show.

Everywhere I turned, there was some form of naked body on display. My eyes were drawn to the beautiful woman spread-eagled and strapped to the giant spinning wheel, her naked body covered in a sheen of sweat and desire. Her partner had her upside down as he ate her out, her pussy at the right height for him not to have to bend down. I watched as her mouth fell open and another orgasm ripped through her. I wondered how many she had endured already when her partner stood back and spun the wheel around a few times until she was upright and facing him. He licked the sweat from her pussy all the way up between her breasts, over her throat and chin, and kissed her like he wanted to devour her as he inserted a vibrator. And so began their routine again.

To the left of the stage, another naked woman was attached to ropes, like a puppet. The ropes supported her weight as her routine partner fucked her from behind. I could see the redness where the ropes dug into her flesh. My eyes were transfixed on her partner's huge cock as he pulled out and teased her entrance before slowly inserting it back in.

A deep voice interrupted my ogling. "Dance with me."

I turned to look up at my masked suitor. "Colton, I know it's you. I can see your neck tattoo."

"I wasn't trying to disguise myself." He licked his white-painted lips, and the contrast of his red tongue had me staring at his mouth.

"I can't." I turned back to the stage and watched the puppet now get fucked in the mouth.

Colton moved closer then. His chest brushed my arm, and a cold shiver escaped over my skin. "Anything goes here, Murdoch. There are no rules. And no one else will fucking touch you in here." He whispered against the sensitive area on my neck.

I flinched at his last words and turned back to stare at him in "What the fuck is that supposed to mean?"

"Work it out." A deep chuckle rumbled in his chest. Unlike the others, his was not playful. On Colton, it sounded dangerous and depraved.

I swallowed hard. "I'm not dancing with you." I tried to sound convincing, but even I noticed the undertone in my voice. The atmosphere in here had my mind in a mess. My senses were heightened, and all the sex in the air had started to eat away at my ability to think straight.

Colton gripped my hand and dragged me to the dancefloor. "I like a challenge. Don't fight me." He pulled me into him and held me firmly against him.

As much as I wanted to hate the closeness, I didn't. I tried to get out of his vice-like grip, but his fingers dug into my side. "Colton, we can't. Someone will see." I looked up into his devastating eyes and knew I was fucked. This was all sorts of fucked up.

"No secrets leave this place, Peyton. I could bend you over right here and slide my hard dick into your tight pussy and no one would say a fucking thing." His hand slid over my ass as we swayed to the music. His filthy words sent heat straight between my legs.

I could feel myself losing control and I fucking hated it. "We need to stop." I pressed my hands against his chest.

He grabbed my hand in his and leaned down until his face was against mine. "It all goes back to normal tomorrow. Don't you want to see where your fantasies take you?" His evil chuckle vibrated against my skin.

I felt someone press against my back, and I jerked my head into their chest.

"Go with it, Peyton. Lose yourself." Colton grabbed my two arms and positioned them around the neck of the person behind me.

I looked up to see Tyler stare back at me.

His eyes sparkled with lust as he pressed his hardness into my ass. The heat and the thumping music overtook my ability to think straight, and I closed my eyes for a moment. Hands roamed my breasts and the pressure against my ass had the ache in my pussy become almost unbearable that I found myself grinding against Colton.

"Spread your legs," Colton growled as his fingers traced their way up my thigh and teased me until I willingly spread my legs enough for his hand to slide between my legs. He lets out a low approving growl as he realized I didn't have any underwear on, and didn't hesitate to start playing torturously with my clit.

A slow and cold fear wrapped itself around my need for release. I was lost in instant ecstasy as his fingers drove deep inside me, and he thrust them in and out in a slow torturous motion. I tipped my head back, and my legs shook as I clenched around his fingers. I held on to Tyler as Colton's fingers circled my clit and teased me until I could barely stand on my own two feet. Tyler's warm lips skated over the sensitive skin of my neck as he pinched my nipples in time with the bass of the music. They both worked me until my legs began to quiver, and sweat poured off me as my orgasm started to build.

"Scream for me," Colton demanded. He pressed his lips against the corner of my mouth and flicked his tongue out.

I shook my head but kept my eyes shut tight. Colton's expert fingers hit the spot just as Tyler bit down on the apex of my neck. "Fuck!" I growled, as the orgasm I so desperately needed convulsed through me and I blacked out.

Coming to moments later, I looked up into the satisfied smirk on Colton's face. Tyler still roamed his hands up and down my sides, encouraging my hips to follow his in a sultry dance. While I watched Colton stared into my eyes and licked his fingers clean.

"I need a drink." Colton suddenly stepped back and made his way to the bar. I followed his movements with my eyes as he disappeared, I was equally blissed out and confused as I tried to pull my thoughts back in order.

Tyler continued to encourage my body to move with his. Working me up into a state that shouldn't be possible after the orgasm I'd just had. He stopped dancing suddenly and led me to a couch in a dark corner. He sat down and pulled me onto his lap, my back to his chest so I couldn't see his face.

Tyler waved over one of the servers and motioned for them to bring us drinks. They returned shortly after with two classes of clear liquid with ice. I eyed the glasses with caution and hesitated, only taking one after Tyler had.

"It's water," the waiter stated, giving me a matter of fact look.

I held the glass in my hands, not trusting it.

"Here," Tyler threw me back so I was half laying down, cradled in his strong arm. I nearly lost the contents of my glass from the sudden movement. "Open for me." He took a sip of his drink and leaned into me, his eyes intent on my mouth.

"Wait." I tried to sit back up when his soft lips connected with mine and he let the liquid trickle into my mouth. It was the fucking sexiest thing ever, and I swallowed the drink without even thinking. Like this was the most natural and sexual way to consume liquid.

His lips lingered on mine, as he ran his cold tongue along my overheated lips before he moved so he could see me better. "More?" He waggled his eyebrows.

I grinned up at him, unable to contain the sudden heat that coursed through me. "I'm good," I said, a little disappointed. I wanted him to put his lips back on me, but I fought the urge and sat back up.

I took a slow sip of my drink, and the lemon in the water sent a tang to my taste buds that wasn't altogether pleasant and most definitely nowhere near as good as the liquid from his lips. Despite this, I was so thirsty, that I managed to finish the glass in a few short gulps.

"You look fucking sexy tonight," Tyler murmured against my neck.

"What do you want here, Tyler?" I didn't have the patience for his games.

"Aren't we all here to live out our deepest, darkest fantasies? Without question or consequence." I froze, his words striking me in a way that spread a cold chill over my body. Without another word, he ran his hand up my exposed thigh, parted the slit in my dress, and stroked agonizingly slow languid lines from my knee to just below where I was suddenly desperate for him to touch. His movements made my body relax, and I gave into him against my better judgment.

"Boss man wouldn't like this," he mumbled seductively, as his hands finally moved to start rubbing circles around my clit, dipping into my juices to bring them back up and start his torturous circling again. I could feel my second orgasm of the night start to build, just as Tyler plunged two fingers straight into me. His expert fingers curving to hit just right, making me arch my back into him with a moan I couldn't hold in.

"That's it, Peyton, give in to me."

He lifted his other hand and started to swirl his fingers around my nipple through the dress, sending bolts straight to my suddenly neglected clit. Only for him to press his palm right there, rubbing against my clit while his fingers slid in and out of me at a torturously slow pace.

"I'm going to take it from you tonight because I know you won't give it to me yet," Tyler said, almost too low for me to hear.

He started kissing my neck while picking up speed with his fingers. He bit down almost to the edge of pain and sent me flying into my orgasm. The heat started at my feet, and the tingles flowed throughout my body, sending me into a state of bliss. I knew I'd completely drenched Tyler's hand with my release; I could feel it.

After I came down from my high and got control of my legs, I got up from Tyler's lap.

"What do you think you're doing?" He had a look of determination on his face, unwilling to let me just walk away.

"I need the ladies' room. I don't want to walk around dripping down my legs all night!" I turned and caught the look of the devil pass through his eyes.

I made my way toward a dark hallway that led to the bathrooms. After a few moments, I started to feel unsteady on my feet but assumed it was the after-effects of my two orgasms.

I managed to get to the bathrooms, clean myself up, and wash my hands before I started to feel fuzzy. I needed to find Capri, as I wasn't feeling too hot. I made my way back down the dark hall. I could barely walk straight and found myself bouncing from side to side off the narrow hallway. I blinked rapidly to clear my blurry vision before I stumbled into the wall and my eyes caught a dark shadow.

A tall figure loomed at the end of the hall

and slowly crept their way toward me, those same eerily familiar eyes shining back at me. I wanted to tell them to fuck off, but my voice got lost in the pounding of my head. The last thing I saw was a golden skull mask before I collapsed to the ground, and everything went dark.

CHAPTER TWELVE

Peyton

"Peyton. Peyton. Wake up, babe."

I felt a deep ache in my bones. An ache like nothing I had ever experienced before. It felt as though my head was about to erupt. I was chilled to the bone, my left side numb from the rough surface under me. The sharp edges dug into my flesh.

"Peyton. Fuck. Someone help me get her inside!" Capri's voice sounded like an echo in the distance.

Her hand gripped my arm as she tried to haul me up. I protested, "Wait, let me sit up."

I blinked my eyes open to come face to face with Capri's smudged skull face paint. "What happened?" I pushed myself up off the brick steps as Capri helped me to sit. The world around me still spun slightly.

"Are you okay?" Capri gripped my shoulders and made me look at her. "Peyton."

"I think so." I allowed my eyes to look past Capri, and I spotted St. Ivy uniforms gathered at the sides of the gate. "What the fuck is going on?" My hands flew to my chest, and I glanced down to see I was still dressed in last night's red dress.

The sound of whispers and giggles echoed in my ears as the other students all stared at me. "Got a fucking problem?" I shouted in anger just as the three assholes arrived and strolled past without even a glance my way. I grabbed a stone closest to me and pegged it at Tyler's back. He looked right through me as though last night didn't happen. "Fuck you." I flipped him the finger as he kept walking to the school entry.

Typical fucking male. I was so done with them.

"Come on, get up." Capri hauled me to my

feet and helped me up the stairs toward the girls' bathrooms, her arm wrapped snuggly around my waist since I was still slightly off-kilter.

I felt dizzy and nauseated the further I walked, and I was glad to be dragged into one of the cubicles with a shower. I sat my confused ass down on the bench seat and let Capri take charge.

"Get two sets and bring them into B Block bathrooms. Thanks, babe." Capri ended the phone call and squatted down in front of me. "Peyton, where the fuck did you get to? I've been out all night looking for you." She placed her head in her hands.

"I don't know. Why are you still in your dress too?" I brushed her hair away from her face. She looked like a mess. Probably not as bad as me, but she looked as though she had traipsed through the woods.

"I lied to your mom and said we were staying at one of my friend's houses. I've been out all night with Jasper, driving through the town and searching on the beach for you. You just disappeared." She sobbed. "I thought something bad happened."

"I'm so sorry. The last thing I remember is dancing with Tyler and-." My voice cut off, and I couldn't get his name out.

Capri met my gaze with her own. "I know. I saw you."

"Oh my god." I buried my face in my hands and wished the shower drain would open up and swallow me whole.

She pried my hands away from my face. "I don't care if you and Colton have a thing." She screwed up her face in disgust.

"There is no *thing.*" I shook my head in disbelief at what I allowed myself to do last night. "But after I danced with them, and Tyler and I...never mind. I went to the bathroom and then nothing."

"Nothing?" Capri looked up at me, her face covered in a smudge of black and white face paint.

I sat and wracked my brain for answers. "The last thing I saw was a golden skull mask, but that could have been anyone." I sighed in frustration.

"Was it painted or a mask?" Capri sat on the floor and crossed her legs.

"I had a hard time seeing by then, and I

honestly couldn't tell the difference." I bent down and took off both my heels. My feet felt instantly better.

Capri tilted her head. "Did you drink?"

"Only some lemon water Tyler got brought over to us." I went over the events of the night and tried my fucking damnedest not to think of their hands on me. "Holy shit!" I jumped up and punched the cubicle wall. "Someone spiked the drink the waiter brought over. Who the fuck does this shit?" I was so fucking angry, I wanted to storm out of the bathrooms, find Tyler, and pummel his face in.

"Are you sure?" Capri massaged her temples.

"Capri, are you in here?" a low voice called from the main bathroom area.

"In here." Capri got up and opened the cubicle door. "Thanks, babe. Keep Mrs. Thompson occupied if we don't make it to chemistry on time." She grabbed the two school bags with fresh uniforms inside from Katie.

"Are you two okay? Do you need me to do anything?" Katie eyed us both with concern.

"The uniforms are plenty. You've saved our

asses." Capri closed the cubicle door as Katie left the bathrooms.

"I have no underwear," I stated, my voice flat and monotone.

"Me either. But it's either this or getting detention, and we don't need your mom finding out about this." Capri raised her eyebrows at me and extended a school bag my way.

"You've got a valid point." I gratefully took the bag and placed it on the bench seat.

"Are you okay to shower by yourself? I mean, do you feel fine?" Capri eyed me suspiciously like I was about to lie to her.

"I'll give it a go. I'll call out to you if I don't feel good." I smiled and let her leave the cubicle to get herself cleaned up.

I stripped off my dress and stood under the steaming hot water as it cascaded over my aching body. I turned and let the spray wash over my face. The sting was a sobering reminder of the pain I planned on dishing out to the fuckers who did this to me. I pumped out the shower gel and lathered it up in my hands, proceeding to scrub the skull off my face and any remnants of last night I could manage. My anger was fueled the longer I lathered myself and the more the images of last night flashed inside my head.

I rinsed myself off and managed to keep most of my hair dry, and turned off the shower. I inspected my skin for any marks or reminders of what might have happened to me while I was fucking out of it.

Nothing.

Not a single new bruise or mark. Only my scars were evident, and my stomach sunk. I hoped to fucking god they didn't see them last night. I pulled on the crisp new uniform for which I was so grateful and exited the cubicle to spot Capri drying her hair under the hand dryers.

"Katie grabbed some shoes for us too." Capri pointed to the chair in the corner.

"Where did she get all this?" I wondered as I walked to grab a pair of low-cut Doc Martens.

"We have spare uniforms in a shared locker. You know, just in case someone gets dirty." Capri winked at me and stepped up to the mirror to check she had removed all the skull paint.

"Dirty." I laughed and placed the shoes on

the floor to slide my feet into them. They fit perfectly, but then again Capri, and I were the same sizes in everything but bras.

"Show me your face." She grabbed my chin between her fingers and moved my head from side to side. "You got it all off. We need to fix your hair." She pushed me down on the chair and went about undoing my braid.

Within ten minutes, my hair was in a top knot, and we both were dressed and on our way to class just as it was about to start. As we headed for our seats, I noticed we both had a notebook and pens ready waiting for us. I mouthed a thank you to Katie, who winked back and smiled. I didn't know what magic Capri and her friends were made of, but I loved them all the more for it.

"Right, class. The school's computer system is down now, so thank your lucky stars for those of you who forgot your laptops. I've organized for us to watch The Martian." Mrs. Thompson looked at us gleefully, fully aware we were not keen on the movie. "I know, the movie sucks, but it was the only one I could think of on such short notice that has any chemistry in it. Who knows what I'm referring to?" She waited for someone to answer.

After a few moments of silence, I decided to answer her. "When he makes water from rocket fuel."

The class turned to stare at me like I was some sort of freak. I caught Hawke's gaze as his eyes narrowed briefly, and then he winked at me like he had a hidden agenda I wasn't understanding. What the fuck was his issue?

"Perfect, Miss. Murdoch. Consider yourself with a few extra points for the end of the week pop quiz." She clapped, and the class groaned.

I returned my gaze to the screen at the front of the classroom and wondered if Colton had found the artwork I'd drawn just for him. I chuckled to myself as the movie started, and I settled in for a relaxing lesson, which was just what I needed to recharge myself before I faced off with Tyler.

All things considered, I felt pretty good for someone that had been drugged the night before. I knew from experience that I hadn't been fondled with, and as fucked up as that was, I was very fucking relieved.

About halfway through the film, a student knocked on the door and entered to speak with

Mrs. Thompson. In their hand was a black envelope that they refused to hand over to the teacher. Mrs. Thompson looked extremely annoyed that she had to get up and pause the film to allow the student to hand over the note.

"Sorry, class, apparently this student needs to hand this note straight to its rightful recipient." Mrs. Thompson folded her arms across her chest and waited.

The male student stood at the front of the classroom and scanned the students in attendance. "Owen Miller, you have been notified." He stood and held out the black envelope to a highly nervous Owen.

Whispered voices snaked across the classroom as students stared at Owen make his way to the front of the classroom. I looked to Capri for answers, but her eyes were fixed on the student at the front of the classroom. I followed her line of sight and was met with two dark eyes staring back at me. Eyes that seemed creepily familiar yet so hauntingly distant.

Owen returned to his seat as the student left the classroom, and Mrs. Thompson turned the film back on. The rest of class went by without another interruption, and once it was over, some students hovered around Owen's desk to find out what was in his envelope. I spotted Hawke hovering outside the classroom door as I exited, thinking he would dish out some shit, but he barely acknowledged me and kept his gaze on Owen.

Capri headed to her next class, and I made my way to study hall. I detoured toward the cafeteria to get a coffee and something to eat. My stomach was in knots from being ravenously hungry thanks to not eating for what felt like fucking forever. As I made my way toward the hall leading to the cafeteria, I happened upon something sinister. I stopped to listen just outside the open door of the utility room the cleaners used to store their equipment in. The room was still dark, so I knew whoever was in there didn't want to be heard or seen. Shouldn't have left the door open, dipshit.

"What the fuck did I tell you?" a deep voice seethed. The venom in their tone could poison their victim with the sound alone.

"I didn't," the other male voice argued back, and I heard a sharp thwack.

"Don't fucking backchat. You know you fucked up."

"He fucked up. I kept my part," the guy defended himself.

"Make sure this time you finish this. I want it clean. I want it quiet. Don't make me send my three to assist you."

Without another word, a student dressed in his preppy St. Ivy uniform exited the utility room with blood dripping from the corner of his mouth. He stormed past me and nearly knocked me over in his haste.

"Watch where you're walking." I steadied myself and turned back toward the doorway to see Colton leaning on the door jamb. He clocked my expression, and his cocky grin in return was as calm and collected as the rest of him.

"Peyton," he purred. He stood with his arms crossed, tattooed forearms on delicious display, and a sinister smirk on his lips.

I didn't think I would see him this soon after last night, and my insides were still in turmoil. "I'm late for study hall." I went to leave, but I was rooted to the spot when he popped the ball of his tongue ring out and slid it across his bottom lip. Unnerved by the way my heart rate sped up, I pretended like I didn't see it. And I sure as fuck didn't notice it when he had his tongue down my throat.

His gaze darkened as he watched me. "That's the extent of what you want to say to me?"

My instincts were all off. Colton Knight was no preppy rich boy living in his daddy's world; he was sin and depravity wrapped in evil glares and wicked touches. His black-rimmed glasses and his rich boy antics hid the true monster beneath.

"I thought I signed my rights away to talk about last night before I entered." I threw my words at him like a barbed spike.

I had the full intensity of his attention, and it caused the base of my throat to close up. "You did. But I was referring to a few moments ago." His leer would have made me run months ago.

"What? You smacking a student around like your three best friends?" I accused him.

His dark sneer caught me off guard as he lunged for me, knocking the wind out of me when I hit the wall. His muscular chest held me in place, and the depraved and fucked up parts of me liked it. I liked that he didn't treat me like a broken shell. I liked that he wasn't gentle and careful around me. I hated him and wanted him in equal parts.

My body betrayed me by sending a flush across my face, and his menacing eyes caught it. "Don't stick your nose where it doesn't belong. You'll end up getting hurt," he growled.

I glared at him. "Is that a threat?"

"It's a warning." His tone lowered, and there was nothing but dominance in his words. It pierced through me and sent a rush of heat and wanting to my core. His eyes lingered on my mouth until we both heard giggles echo down the hall. "Fuck. Get to class." He pushed off me, stormed the opposite way, and left a sense of foreboding in the air.

I eyed the seniors as I waltzed past and pretended like nothing was out of the ordinary.

"You know, he fucks anything that walks. Ask Stass; she's been bent over his desk so many times I'm surprised it doesn't have an imprint of her tits in it," one of the guys teased.

I threw him a death glare and took the high road, heading to study period. Even though for some fucked up reason, his remark stung and ate at my insides. This jealousy shit needed to end.

After the stress-free and calm study period, I was busting to pee and hurried to the nearest girls' bathrooms. I huffed as I pushed my way into the bathroom, thankful they were mostly empty. There was nothing worse than having to walk through masses of girls primping and priming their appearances just to do your business. I closed myself into the nearest free stall and pulled my skirt up to sit and pee.

I heard shuffling, and a muttered, "Fuck." The girl was in the stall next to mine. I paused and listened to make sure it wasn't some horn bag who couldn't wait until the end of school to get their rocks off. You'd be surprised how many students hook up here in the bathrooms.

"Fuck. Fuck. Fuck!" This time the muttered curses were more distressed.

"Are you okay?" I whispered. The voice seemed familiar, but it was hard to tell with the wall between us.

"Um, yep, just fucking great. Of course, I would get my period when I don't have any tampons." Her strained voice echoed through the room.

I knew that feeling all too well of being caught short at that time of the month. No woman should ever have to go without. You'd think at a ritzy school like this, they'd provide them for free. They probably had better things to spend their money on, like paying off the police to keep their mouth shut.

I pulled a fresh packet of tampons from the school bag Katie had supplied me, glad there were some spare in there and handed them under the stall wall. "Here."

"Thanks heaps, girlfriend. You just totally saved me!" I could hear the relief in her voice.

I didn't say anything in reply. Not wanting to make a big deal out of it. I finished peeing and exited to wash my hands. The door opened, and of course, Miss Queen Bee stepped out. She froze on the spot, staring at me warily. Like she was waiting for me to make something out of me helping her.

I washed and dried my hands, giving her a small smile in the mirror. She didn't smile back. She just stood there and stared at me. I placed the hand towel in the container under the sink and left the bathroom to give her privacy.

Capri caught my arm as I left the bathroom, linking us together. "I'm starving!" She exclaimed.

"Same," I replied as we headed for the cafeteria. I piled my plate high with deep-fried chicken, coleslaw, and mashed potatoes. I was fucking ravenous, and I didn't give a shit that the other students looked at me like I'd grown a second head. If one of them made one more fucking remark, I was happy to paint their face with mash and make them choke on a drumstick.

"Are you feeling okay?" Capri grabbed a drumstick off my plate and started eating it.

"I am." I turned to her. "Thanks for saving my ass. I owe you." I gripped her around the neck and kissed her cheek.

"Have you heard?" Katie slid in beside me and stole another drumstick.

"Heard what?" Capri and I answered in unison.

"The rumor around school is that Mr. Knight has been fucking students in his office." Katie's eyes lit up.

Capri eyed me, and I suddenly could barely stomach the mash and gravy that I had just shoveled in my mouth. I shook my head slightly to let her know it wasn't me, but the thought of him with another student made my insides churn.

"Eww, stop." Capri placed her hands over her ears in mock horror.

I didn't want to listen to this anymore, and I stood to leave. Hunger be damned.

"Where are you going?" Capri worried, her hand resting on my arm.

"I just lost my appetite." I forced a smile and pretended the news made me feel the same sick in the stomach as Capri. But in truth, I was fucking enraged and insanely jealous. Fuck. I had to get it together. He touched me three times now, and that did not make him in any way, shape, or form mine.

"Want me to come with you?" Capri offered, but I declined.

I headed for the bathrooms as I needed to splash my face with cold water and get a fucking grip. I gripped the handbasin as my anger and jealousy simmered inside me. I stared at my reflection. The dark circles around my eyes showed the only signs of last night. I looked so fucking tired. I turned the faucet on and held my hands under the running water before I splashed my face to help ease my rage.

"She said he also took her out last night on a date. Like a real motherfucking date date," a whiny voice echoed in my ears.

"Mr. Knight? Are you for real?" giggled another girl.

I twisted to see two senior girls standing by the full-length mirror by the entrance. I turned the faucet off and cracked my neck. This shit had to end. "She's lying," I said, my tone dead.

Both snobby girls turned and wrinkled up their noses at me. Yes, I had no makeup on, and my hair was a mess, but they just looked that way at the wrong fucking person. "What the fuck would you know?" The brunette with short hair laughed.

"She's lying," I repeated.

Brunette two with the longer hair, tilted her head at me. "Go back to the hole you crawled out of, charity case." Her eyes gave me a once over before she turned back to fixing her perfect fucking hair in the mirror.

Something inside me snapped, and I lunged at her and gripped her perfect mane of brunette hair at the nape of her neck before smashing her face into the mirror. Blood instantly splattered on the glass as the crunch of her nose echoed in the small room. A choked cry spluttered from her mouth, and her hands flew up to grip mine. Her friend stood stock still, in shock, no doubt, and did fucking nothing to help save her friend.

"Want to spread more shit about people?" I yanked on her hair, and she nearly tripped over backward.

She didn't respond; she just started crying like a fucking baby and cupping her bleeding nose in her trembling hands. I let go of her and retreated as I came back down from my rage. I needed to escape, so I headed for the old stone building at the back of the school, hoping that Frankie would be there and I could lay low until the end of school.

Fuck, this was going to be bad. My mom was going to kill me if she found out.

CHAPTER THIRTEEN

Peyton

I leaned against the sink basin as the shower water heated and the steam started to fill the room. Everything in this room was too expensive. Too shiny. Just another reminder that none of it was truly mine. I was forever living my life for someone else, by the rules of someone else.

As the anger in me rose, so did the pressure inside. I could feel it pound in my heart, my head, constricting me like it always did when they took control. I could feel the walls closing in and the tightness in my body becoming agonizingly unbearable.

One more time wouldn't hurt. One more beautiful scar to release the pressure inside and give me the control that was always stolen from me. But they couldn't steal this. This was mine. My scars. My most cherished secret. The only thing I had that was truly mine. My own form of blissful control.

I stepped into the shower and let the burning hot water cascade over my body for a few moments before I grabbed the loofah and scrubbed my body, leaving it red and angry. I scrubbed my hair clean to try to clear my overwhelming thoughts.

It wasn't enough.

Thoughts of hopelessness, anger, sexual tension, and frustration invaded my brain. I couldn't handle the pressure any longer. I'd been strong enough for too long. I'd pretended for too long. For just one moment, I needed to feel vulnerable.

To feel real.

To feel that relief.

To feel like me again.

I reached out of the shower into the drawers and found my favorite knife. My stunning rose gold knife with a marble swirl on the handle. The swirl pattern reminded me of the patterns of my blood as it ran down my leg and mixed with the water to create the most beautiful form of art.

I moved to the edge of the shower and admired my artwork on my hip, and marveled at the beauty of my own control. I brought the blade to my skin and pressed it just deep enough to break the skin, to allow the blood to slowly seep from the beautiful line I left behind.

I could finally take my first free breath in weeks. As I watched the blood glisten and seep from my skin, I felt the pressure inside me slowly drain with it. Like it was released directly from that magical spot. It gave me a pain I could focus on, a pain I could control.

I paused and waited for the prickling numbness to take over my body as the release of endorphins slowly seeped through me. The slow build of tingling began in my fingers and toes and spread throughout my body in the most intoxicating relief. It lifted the weight from my chest and the pressure from my head. I watched as the blood mixed with the water and created patterns down my leg and swirled in magical circles on the shower floor before it disappeared down the drain along with my anxiety.

I rested my head on the shower wall and let the hot water crash over me until the blood stopped oozing out of my cut. I turned the shower off and stepped out to grab an overly soft and fluffy towel to dry myself. I wrapped the towel around me and headed for my chest of drawers, where I hid a first aid kit for these moments. I searched through it until I found a dry dressing to tape over my latest addition.

I heard noises from downstairs, but even the reminder of the reality that awaited me outside this room couldn't bring me down. I felt invincible.

I pulled on my tiny denim shorts that barely covered my ass and an oversized navy-blue St. Ivy hoodie I'd found in my clean wash basket the maid had left in my room earlier. I padded down the stairs and set about finally making my first coffee for the day, seeing as I hid in the Club House with Frankie until school was over. Capri and I had scored a lift home with Katie, and no one mentioned the bathroom incident, so I kept my mouth shut.

Capri was at Jaspers, and the house was eerily quiet for this time of day. I made my coffee, grabbed a bag of crisps, and headed out the back to go sit on the beach for a while. As I meandered through the manicured gardens and past the pool, I couldn't help but casually stroll past the pool house. Because I liked to fuck with my own emotions. My heart started to race, and I tried to walk past quickly when I heard him behind me.

"Heard you were defending my honor." His voice cut through me like glass.

I hesitated, and part of me wanted to keep walking, but the snarkier part of me was ready for a verbal match. So, I turned around and faced him and wished I hadn't.

Holy fuck.

He was in low-slung black basketball shorts and nothing else, granting me the perfect view of his sweaty, muscled torso. The tattoos I found myself fantasizing about were on perfect display now. My eyes scanned his chest, and the tattoo inked there was written in a language I couldn't read. I allowed my hungry gaze to drop to the defined v where a number

5 sat center stage right above his cock. I bit my lip at that thought and dragged my eyes back over his muscled abs, and admired the shiny barbel in his nipple.

"Lost for words. I mustn't be doing my job properly. Do you need private lessons?" A deep chuckle rolled through him.

My eyes snapped to his, and the hungry look he threw at me set my blood on fire. I swallowed the heat that rose up my chest and wanted to char me from the inside. "The bitch shouldn't run her mouth when it's not the truth."

He cocked his head to the side, and the corner of his mouth turned up slightly. "How do you know it's not the truth?" The humor was long gone from his voice.

I felt my heart slam against my chest, and the urge to throw my hot coffee in his face was strong. My fingers tightened around the mug as my insides felt like they'd been ripped apart. "Fuck you, Colton," I managed to grit out before I turned on my heels and started toward the beach again.

"Jealousy is a curse." The rumble of his lowered voice shook me.

He knew how to rile me up, and of course, I took the bait because I could never just walk the fuck away from anything. I spun on the spot, and my coffee splashed over my hand and burned my skin. "What the fuck is there to be jealous about?" I looked him up and down and cocked an eyebrow.

He folded his massive biceps across his chest, and all of a sudden, he seemed bigger than usual. "Is that my fucking hoodie you're wearing?" he accused.

I looked down and realized it was obscenely big on me. "Clara put it in my laundry basket." I looked up at him.

"I'll have it back, thanks," he challenged.

I narrowed my eyes at him. Was he for real? "Now?"

He nodded in response and kept his hot gaze on me.

I strode up to him and pushed my coffee mug into his abs. "Hold this." The hot liquid splashed over his muscles, but he didn't as much as flinch. He took the mug from me and waited. I threw the crisps onto the ground in anger and gripped the hem of his hoodie before furiously pulling it over my body.

Once I had dislodged my arms from the sleeves, I yanked my mug back, not that there was much coffee left in it, and threw his hoodie in his face. "There's your fucking hoodie. Satisfied?" I spat.

He held back a smirk and pulled his bottom lip between his teeth as his eyes dropped to my tits. I hadn't put on a bra after my shower and all I had on was a see-through baby pink singlet, which I'm sure left nothing to the imagination.

"Very." His eyes darkened to a sinister shade.

I bent down, which was probably the dumbest thing to do, to pick up the crisps and went to storm off. I was so pissed by this point I wanted to hit something.

"Not so fast." His arm flicked out, and he hooked his two fingers into the top of my denim shorts, yanking me into him. My coffee splashed about and covered both of us. Heat licked up my body from his touch and stirred the burning flames of my desire once more.

Colton began to walk backward into the pool house, dragging me with him. I had no choice but to stumble into him on my tiptoes and be led into the wolf's den. My coffee and crisps were left in a heap on the grass. His sinister gaze bounced from my mouth to my eyes and back until we were inside. Without letting go of the front of my shorts, he reached around me with his free hand and slammed the door shut. The loud bang echoed around the room.

"Colton-" I started before he cut me off.

"Did I say you could talk?" He placed his pointer finger on my lips to stop me and raised a brow challenging me to back away.

The lingering scent of his cologne mixed with the sweet musk of his sweat had me nearly throwing myself at him. The rush of adrenaline that coursed through me at the thought of what we were doing made me dizzy. This forbidden and off-limits man made me fucking crazy. My heart thudded against my chest so hard that I could guarantee he could feel it too.

"Tell me you're jealous." Colton leaned down and nipped the sensitive skin at the top of my shoulder.

I fought against the desires that throbbed in my clit. "No," I said, defiant as ever.

His hot breath fanned across my cheek as

he moved to my earlobe and sucked it into his mouth, circling and flicking and pressing his tongue ring against it. He moved slightly, and the distance was too much. "You know where else this would feel good?" He sucked my earlobe back into his hot mouth.

My breath quivered as I sharply inhaled a lungful of air. My eyes closed, and I was lost in the heat that ran through me as he teased my ear. He moved again and towered over me, his gaze a fireball of desire and destruction. But I didn't care. Right at this point, I didn't care how much he'd destroy me. I wanted him. I wanted all of him.

"Tell me you're jealous," he growled, his eyes turning to ice.

"Fine. I'm fucking jealous," I bit back, trying to step away from him.

His hand, still hooked in the top of my shorts, stopped me possessively. "Where the fuck do you think you're going?" His free hand landed on the area just above my ass and sent electric currents through me.

I gripped his arms, finding they were as hard as rock under my fingertips. My eye line was in the perfect position to admire the barbell in his nipple, and I bit the inside of my lower lip to stop myself from letting out a quiet moan.

My head jerked up to look at him, and what stared back at me made me instantly aroused and slightly nervous.

His sharp jaw twitched. "That's right. Nowhere," He said with a feral growl.

I took in a sharp breath at the arrogance of his words. "Colton," I tried again, but my words caught in my throat. I didn't know if I deliberately didn't argue with him because I needed this as much as I needed my next breath or because I was being a fucking wimp and about to chicken out.

His ocean green eyes burned into me as he pulled me further into the pool house until we were in his bedroom doorway. He didn't even pause for a second. He dragged me far enough in before he spun us on the spot so he could kick the door closed.

"No backing out now, Murdoch." His tone changed to something sinister as he grabbed me around the hips and hauled me over his shoulder, slapping my ass for emphasis. The sting of his hand on me sent heat to my clit.

He threw me onto the bed and watched my tits bounce as the mattress moved under my weight, my hard nipples pressing against the sheer fabric of my singlet. My gaze lingered on his basketball shorts, which did nothing to hide his hard dick. I licked my lips unknowingly and heard an evil low chuckle as Colton climbed up the bed and hovered over me. The veins in his forearms stuck out, and his hair had fallen forward in a sexy as fuck way. I bit my lip to stop myself from squirming under him.

"I'm going to break you, Murdoch." His gaze dipped to my tits, and an appreciative growl rumbled in his chest. "Take your clothes off," he ordered.

"You first," I taunted him.

He jumped off the bed in a second flat, and my heart almost stopped beating at the empty feeling he left behind. I wanted to tell him exactly what I thought, that he was a giant prick, but I watched in fascination as his huge fucking dick sprung free when he removed his shorts.

"Your turn, Murdoch." He gripped the length of his dick in his hand and started stroking it.

Heat pulsed in my pussy, and I swallowed thickly as my eyes glued to his hand movements. I sat up on the bed and pulled my singlet off, tossing it to the side before undoing my denim shorts and throwing them with my singlet. I hesitated with my hands on my panties.

"Too late to be shy now." Colton moved swiftly, a predatory grunt escaping his lips as he pinned me under him. I felt the hardness of his erection dig into my stomach.

I was fucking thirsty for this man, and it was almost embarrassing. The thrill of this being so taboo and illicit made me hungry for him.

He grazed my lips with his teeth before he crashed his mouth to mine, devouring me. The kiss was raw and brutal, and his firm grip on my hip was painful from where I had cut myself earlier. He dragged his lips down my neck and over my breast, pausing to bite my hard nipple, the pain almost unbearable.

"Holy fuck," I cried out, digging my nails into his shoulders.

He moved further down my body as he

grazed his teeth over my sensitized skin until he reached my panties. "Lift your ass." He breathed against me.

I hesitated, as I didn't want him to see my scars, but with the quick smack to my pussy, I jerked up and almost kicked him. "Oh!" I moaned. The pleasure that coursed through me from that one sharp touch surprised me, and before I could register what was happening, he had my panties around my ankles and on the floor.

A sinful look washed over his features as though the devil had just stepped up to play and I was about to be his sacrifice. He spread my legs as wide as they could go and buried his face in my needy pussy. His tongue drove into me, and he licked up to my clit in one long hard stroke. The cold press of his tongue ring was almost too much.

"Fuck," I whimpered, and my eyes felt like they had rolled into the back of my head as I gripped the sheets.

He pinched my clit with his fingers, and I jerked my eyes open, not prepared for the pleasurable pain he inflicted. His perfect tongue replaced his fingers again, and he sucked and licked in swirls and strokes, the tongue ring sending all sorts of pleasurable mayhem to my senses. Colton groaned against me, and the vibration made me grind against his face as I grabbed his hair in my fists and gritted my teeth trying to hold back my orgasm.

He teased and tormented my pussy until I let out a choked moan as my intense orgasm ripped through me and I was a trembling mess on the bed. I could barely breathe as I sucked in much-needed air and came down from my high.

I hadn't noticed his hand on my dry dressing until it was too late and he had already removed it. He ran his fingers along the fresh wound, and I felt the warm flow of blood as his tongue and lips worked me up to almost losing control again.

"What are you?" I was silenced with a thunderous glare as Colton painted my pussy with my blood and dipped his fingers into me as I pulsated around them.

He removed his fingers from inside me and his tongue replaced them, licking the blood away before he dug his fingernail into my cut again. "Do you like pain, Murdoch?" His voice was harsh and barely audible over my heavy breathing.

I moaned in disgusted pleasure as he played with the cut on my hip the same way he had my clit. His gaze never left mine as he spread my blood over my pussy. He kneeled up and lowered himself between my legs, his dick pressing against my entrance.

He didn't wait for me to adjust; he slammed his fucking big dick straight into me, and it felt like he had ripped me apart.

"Shit." I tensed around him and gripped his arms as he pulled out and slammed into me again.

"You're so fucking wet," he growled into my shoulder as he slowly eased out of me. He braced himself up on his hands and knees and flipped me over in one move. "Ass up, baby." He grabbed my hips and hauled me to my knees, running his fingers over my pussy until his sharp fingernail hit my swollen clit.

I bit down on my lip at the sting but pushed my ass back into him, wanting and needing more.

He fisted my hair and pulled my head back

to elongate my neck before he teased my entrance with his cock. "So hungry for it," he growled as he slowly pushed into me.

His other hand snaked around and gripped my throat to hold me in place as he pounded me from behind. I could feel the tightening of his hand as his release neared. "Fuck, Colton. I can barely breathe," I choked out as his thrusts verged on violent.

The pleasure and pain combined with the need for oxygen had my release rip through me without any remorse.

Without warning, he pulled out and threw me onto my back. I was shocked at his brutal glare; he looked like a demon-possessed. He moved too quickly and shoved his cock, covered in my blood and arousal, deep into the back of my throat, spilling his release. His feral moan filled the air as I clawed at his muscled arms and abs to try to get him out of my throat.

Colton stared down at me as he eased himself out of my mouth. His face was flushed and his abs covered in a sheen of sweat. He held out his hand to help me sit up and without saying a word, I took it.

"Need a drink?" He climbed off the bed and pulled his basketball shorts back on.

I watched the muscles in his back as he twisted to glance back at me before he left the room.

"That'd be great." My voice was scratchy, and I cleared my throat.

"Coke, juice, milk?" He smirked at me as he said that last option.

"Fucking funny. Coke will be fine." I flipped him the finger. I scooted over on the bed to grab my singlet and shorts when I spotted all the blood on the sheets, and my heart slammed into my throat. Realization struck me then that he knew my secret and I felt like I was going to be sick. I quickly shoved my feet through the leg holes of my shorts and yanked my singlet over my head. I had to get out of there. I couldn't handle the knowing look in his eye. That he now knew my secret. With that thought I turned and ran out of the pool house without even a glance at Colton.

On my way back up to the house I noticed a blue silk tie floating from my window. My heart froze as I realized it was the same as the one he had always used when he was being extra depraved. I scurried to my room as sweat poured over my body form the sheer terror of him being here. I tore the fucking ribbon off, it felt like it had seared my skin, and threw it out the window. I didn't have the capacity to deal with that on top of everything right now, but a sick knowing feeling settled in my gut. We were so careful when we came here. Surely they didn't know. Surely he hadn't found me.

CHAPTER FOURTEEN

Peyton

"Please enlighten me on why we had to come to this stupid event?" I cleared my throat as I glared at my mom. My voice had become scratchy after my afternoon activities. Just the thought of it made my blood turn to ice, and I hoped to fuck he wasn't here anywhere.

Mom placed the back of her hand against my forehead. "Are you getting sick, honey?"

"If I say yes, does that mean I can go home?" I smiled at her, and she laughed.

"Fat chance." Her gaze scanned the room, like always, ensuring no one from our past was in attendance.

"Let's go get some food." Capri dragged me away from the main conference room and over to the buffet.

We piled our plates high with desserts and snuck out to the lobby to eat.

"Do you think the rumors about Colton are true?" Capri pressed me for my thoughts.

I shoved a huge piece of chocolate mud cake into my mouth so I didn't have to answer her, and she knew it.

"You've been acting weird all day, babe." She watched me carefully. "I know after last night's bullshit and this morning being left on the school steps with half the school seeing you, you must feel a little off and a bit stabby, but we will get to the bottom of this and kick the asses of whoever did it." Capri went off on a tangent.

"Capri," I half-shouted to get her attention. "I slept with Colton this afternoon." I shoved another huge piece of cake in my mouth and hoped she didn't punch me before I finished it. It was fucking good cake.

"Oh babe, Colton is a giant prick. He's going to hurt you, and then I'm going to have to hurt him." She moved closer to me, and I leaned away as far as I could. Capri held her arms out for me. "Come here, let me give you a sympathy hug."

I burst out laughing. "So, you're not going to punch me?"

"The only person getting punched is Colton." She grinned at me innocently.

I moved into her embrace and leaned on her shoulder. "Want some cake?" I offered.

"Was it that bad, huh?" She grabbed the cake and bit a piece off.

"Oh my god." I nearly choked.

"What's so funny ladies?" Tyler planted himself in the seat opposite us.

Hawke and Steele hovered for a few seconds and decided there weren't any better options for company before dropping themselves in the chairs to Tyler's right. They all looked fucking hot, in expensive tuxes, with matching shirts and pink ties. If I wasn't so angry at Tyler for last night's spiked drink saga, I'd probably have allowed my eyes to linger on him a little longer.

"I need to talk to you." I stood abruptly and pointed my finger in his face.

He raised his eyebrow at me, threw me one of his cocky grins, and I almost caved. He stood next to me at full height, and even with my heels on, he was so much fucking taller than me. "Ladies first." He gestured with his hand.

I glanced back at Hawke and Steele, who both looked between me and Tyler in confusion. Capri slapped me on the ass as I made my way outside the hotel lobby with Tyler hot on my heels. The cool night air made my nipples hard, and I caught Tyler's appreciative stare.

"What the fuck?" I pushed at his chest in anger.

He stepped back from my shove and caught my hand in his. "Don't be like that, Bambi." He tried to kiss my hand, but I yanked it out of his grip.

"Are you fucking kidding me?" I pushed him again, only this time he didn't move. His expression turned to confusion as he tried to work out what the fuck I was going on about.

He cocked his head to the side. "Sweet pea, you're the one who disappeared after you came all over my fingers. Shouldn't I be the one with the hurt feelings here?" He stuffed his hands inside his pants pocket. The uncharacteristic raw vulnerability in his voice threw me.

"Someone fucking spiked my drink and I blacked out," I spat at him.

His murderous gaze ate me up and he stepped closer to me, his firm abs pressing against my breasts. "You fucking what?" He seethed.

He looked truly terrifying at that point, and flashes of him holding down the student in the library sent my emotions all over the place. I knew that all of them were part of some fucked up gang or some shit, where they tortured other students for fun. But seeing that side of him, right in front of my face, chilled me to the core. His vicious glare thundered through my conscience, and I became acutely aware of just what it meant to not fuck with them.

"What are you two so heated about?" Colton's voice interrupted us.

I quickly stepped back from Tyler but kept my eyes on him. I couldn't face Colton. I couldn't face him knowing he'd discovered my secret.

Tyler broke the spell and turned to look at

Colton. "Someone fucking drugged her last night."

I heard the sharp intake of Colton's breath as he gripped my arm and turned me to face him. His cold eyes were rimmed with evil fire, a picture out of nightmares, as they landed on me. The twitch of his jaw and the merciless calculated rage that brewed behind his dark ocean eyes made the tips of my ears burn.

"Who the fuck did this?" he growled, the sound animalistic and depraved.

No are you okay? No do you need any help? Nothing but rage emitted from him. My eyes flitted to Tyler, who registered my thoughts.

"Don't fucking look at me. I merely finger fucked you, and then you ran off." He held up his hands innocently.

Colton's grip tightened on my arm, almost possessively, and his glare switched to Tyler. "You let her out of your sights?" Colton's voice turned deadly.

"What the fuck does that mean?" I tried to pull my arm out of Colton's death grip, but he wasn't having a bar of it.

"You three had one job," Colton continued.

"Fuck you, man. She ran off to clean herself

up and then never returned. Steele, Hawke, and I turned that fucking club upside down looking for her."

My stomach started to churn then, as the missing pieces of the puzzle didn't add up. Who the fuck drugged me and what the fuck did they do to me? "What kind of sick fuck gets invited to those parties?" I glared up at Colton.

"Fucking sorry one's," he replied, the dark edge to his voice deadly.

We were interrupted by the screeching of tires as a black SUV stopped on the road a few feet from where we stood. Someone opened the back door and pushed out a female who hit the gutter with a final thud. The SUV, with no plates, roared off down the street and disappeared.

"Fuck," Colton gritted through clenched teeth, letting go of my arm as he and Tyler strode to the female who lay dead still.

I followed behind, and a gasp of shock escaped my lips. The female was still in her St. Ivy uniform. I watched as Colton pushed her to her back with his shiny Armani leather shoe. "Oh fuck," I whispered as her face was revealed. Her eyes were wide open, and they stared blankly up at the dark sky. Her nose was swollen, and dry blood stained her face.

Colton's gaze snapped to me. A knowing smirk turned the corner of his mouth. "This your handy work? I'm honored."

"I didn't fucking kill her. For all I know, it could have been one of you psychos." I wanted to puke. I didn't want the poor girl dead, just to learn a lesson not to spread untrue shit.

"Am I missing something?" Tyler piped up.

"No," I answered quickly, shooting Colton a death glare.

He grinned at me. "Peyton defended my honor and this is the result."

"I didn't fucking do this." I was appalled that he could smile about this. Why was I the only one freaking out?

Colton took out his phone and texted someone. Within seconds, three guys emerged from the party. I spotted Steele and Hawke in the background, hovering by the door. Hawke gave me a knowing look; he always gave me the chills with his unsaid words.

Dressed in their expensive finery, the three guys lifted the dead student by the legs and underarms and carried her away to fuck knows where. I watched Colton as his eyes trailed his minions into the dark. What kind of fucked up games were these guys playing?

"Inside." Colton wrapped his arm around my waist. His thumb brushed over my scars, and the jolt of electricity that coursed through me made me jump.

I should have pried his arm from around me, but to the outside world and unknowing eyes, it only looked like a stepbrother taking care of his stepsister. Steele's dangerous gaze caught me by surprise as he stood by the entrance and flicked his blade in his hands. He had left me alone for the most part, but I knew he had plans to ruin me like he promised that night at the beach.

The three of them followed us back into the lobby and then they all disappeared together. Probably plotting their next victim. I had so many unanswered questions that it made me dizzy. The whole drugging and turning up on the school steps didn't add up. I had a bad feeling that I'd pay for whatever happened while I was out of it.

"Peyton, what the fuck is going on?" Capri found me as I lingered in the lobby.

"It's fucked up. Someone dumped a dead student on the road out there. What's worse, I smashed her face into a mirror at school this morning." I confessed.

Capri's eyebrows shot up. "You what?"

"Fuck." My arms flew to the top of my head, and I started pacing.

"Stop. Breathe." Capri grabbed me by the waist and made me focus on her.

"She was spreading shit about that Stass bitch and Colton, and I guess I just snapped. Fuck, Capri. I haven't snapped in so fucking long." I almost lost it then.

"This is not your fault. Some things go on that no one knows about or can explain." She tried to comfort me with that twisted half-truth.

"You don't say." I wanted to push her for answers, but I knew she didn't have them. "I'm going to go to the bathroom and freshen up."

"No, you're not. You're coming back inside with me." She dragged me into the main conference room.

As we entered I spotted Colton, and the three assholes in a heated conversation with Nathaniel. They all turned to look at me and

Capri, and I got the odd feeling I was about to find out exactly what kind of trouble I was in.

"I need to get out of here," I muttered, turning on my heels, and escaping back out to the lobby.

Capri chased after me. "Peyton, wait."

I stopped and twisted to look at her just as the three assholes appeared in the doorway. I glared at them to make sure they knew my next words were directed at them. "This whole situation is getting more fucked up than I can deal with. I'm going home." My jumbled thoughts were overshadowed by their glares.

"Not going to wait for Colton?" Steele teased, a mean smile touching the corners of his mouth.

I frowned at him. "Why the hell would I do that?"

"Don't want to go for round two of riding his dick? How about letting Tyler make you come back in there? Public is your thing, isn't it?" He was proud of himself; I could see it in the way he puffed his chest out a little.

Fucking asshole.

I threw Tyler an accusatory glare. I couldn't believe he told them all what we did at the stupid secret party. Whatever happened to the 'what happens there, stays there' bullshit we had to sign? And Colton fucking Knight and his big fucking mouth. Maybe the rumors about him and students were true. Maybe I was just another idiot who fell for his shit. I sure as hell wasn't waiting around for Steele to say anything else. I escaped out the door and started on foot down the road. I had no idea where the fuck I was going, I had no plan, I just wanted to go back to the comfort and safety of my room.

"Peyton, hold up!" Tyler shouted, chasing after me. He caught up and stopped in front of me. "Where are you going?"

"None of your business." I tried to shove around him, but he blocked my path.

"Are you seriously chucking a bratty tantrum?"

I glared up at him and wanted to smack the smirk off his face. "I am. So fucking what? Do you four fucking share everything?" I shouted.

His gaze darkened, and his eyes narrowed ever so slightly. "Hey, we're all for sharing you."

I swallowed hard at the thought and pushed

aside my sudden desire to jump him.

"You're thinking about it, aren't you?" He chuckled.

I pushed past him in annoyance. "Don't be stupid." But really, I didn't want him to see the need in my eyes. The need to have them all, as selfish as that was. I knew I hated them to some degree, but a flame ignited deep inside me whenever I was around them.

"I'll give you a lift," he called after me as a limousine pulled up beside me.

The window wound down and sitting inside was Capri. "Get in."

I didn't hesitate for a second. I opened the door and paused to glance at Tyler, who still stood on the sidewalk. He watched me intently. "I'll see you at school," I called out to him, climbing in to sit next to Capri. I left the four of them to deal with the mess I started this morning.

CHAPTER FIFTEEN

Peyton

Colton and the three guys were all MIA at school for the rest of the week, as was Nathaniel from home. I found out after the swanky function that they were away on a business retreat as the founding families of Boat Harbor. Apparently, it was an annual thing and the swanky function I had left early the other night was the beginning of the celebrations. If I was brave enough to admit, I kind of missed the dickheads and their taunts and imposing presence. The school felt almost empty without them.

The day had dragged, especially English class in the morning with the substitute teacher. Even with his asshole ways, Colton was a pretty good teacher, and the rest of the students idolized him. My thoughts, as usual, drifted to him and how he had fucked me the other afternoon. Ever since, it had played over and over in my mind. I needed something to distract me.

After the events of last week, I was glad things had returned to somewhat normalcy. Not a mention of the dead student, yet again. These elite schools sure did look after their own. No leads on who dumped her, and no one questioned me about the altercation in the girls' bathroom. I didn't know where to start with the whole being drugged thing, so I left it on the back burner. I was sure whoever did it would slip up eventually. I just had to bide my time.

With none of the kings to focus on, Maddie had set her prime focus on me. The bitch thought she owned the school just because there wasn't anyone to pull her into line. I stood in front of my locker and pressed the keypad to unlock it, but before I managed that, my face slammed against the hard wooden door.

"What's wrong box dye? Worried no one will want your smashed up little face." Maddie sneered, surrounded by her minions and looked like the cat who had got the cream.

I glared at her, and clenched my fists to stop myself from punching her perfect, fake little nose. "What the fuck are you on about?"

"We all know how much you enjoy being passed around, don't we girls?" Her minions giggled in response.

My blood turned to ice. There was no way any of them knew about my past. I made sure as shit that I'd kept it all hidden. That no one could link my past to here. I sliced my eyes over each of them and their giggling instantly stopped. These bitches knew I'd snap if pushed too far. Their fierce leader hadn't come to the same conclusion and decided to keep running her mouth.

Maddie stepped forward and sized me up. "The whole school knows, Peyton. That you're just creaming to be passed around by the kings, old and new. But guess what, bitch! There's already a queen here, so you can forget claiming that title. Back off from Steele or my daddy will make sure you're broken beyond repair," she growled, jutting her chin out.

I couldn't help but laugh, borderline hysterically. What a fucking joke.

I stepped into her, nudging her backwards with my chest, and got right up in her face. "Listen here, sweetheart. I don't give two fucks about your little royal playtime antics with Steele. You can rule this fucking school. I'm not sticking around this hell hole, I'm getting the fuck out of here once I graduate. As for your daddy issues. Tell him, if he comes near me, I'll make sure the last thing he ever sees is your pretty little head staked on his dick." I watched her ashen face turn white before she scurried off with her minions trailing after her.

My anger bubbled inside me and I flicked my hands to help ease the pins and needles that always appeared whenever I was ready to fight. I turned around and opened my locker to collect my things before I headed home when a piece of thick ivory paper fluttered out. Crimson words stared back at me reading 'Soon, Baby Blue.' My heart stopped as I looked around. Fuck. Did he know I was here?

Dylan would have warned me. He'd never betray me like that. With no other option I took in a calming breath, shoved the fucking note in my bag, and headed home. A dread filled chill following me all the way to the comfort of my room.

It was early Saturday evening when Capri convinced me to go watch Tyler defend his title at an MMA fight night. I hesitated at first, but the temptation to see sexy as fuck men belt each other was way too appealing. As I pulled on my high-waisted leather mini skirt and my cropped white top, I stared at myself in the mirror. I had changed so much in the last eighteen months. The old Peyton was somewhere under all this exterior, and I wondered if I'd ever see her again. I didn't know who this Peyton was that stared back at me. I mean, I tried my fucking hardest to be reserved and not snap at every little thing that pissed me off. I worked hard with my psychologist to get to where I was today, and I was proud. But I longed to be the carefree and fun Peyton of the past. Even for just one evening.

I sighed as I bent down and put on my

mom's vintage cherry red Doc Martens. They didn't match my outfit, but I felt a little like the old me when I wore them.

"Capri, you ready?" I hollered from my room.

"Just putting on my shoes, baby." Her excited voice echoed down the hall before she came barreling in. "Jesus, are you trying to make Tyler lose?"

"What?" I looked at her in confusion.

She looked me up and down. "When he gets one look at you, he won't be able to concentrate."

"Shut up and let's go." I pushed her out of my room and to the garage.

After about forty minutes of driving, we arrived at what looked like a run-down sports stadium. The parking lot was dark, and the lone light that flickered in the far corner barely illuminated the area directly under it. I glanced at Capri and frowned. "If we get mugged, I'm going to kill you."

"We're not getting mugged. Get your ass out of the car. We're late as it is." She pushed at my shoulder to get me to move my ass quicker.

We scurried across the packed parking lot,

paid the entrance fee, and got our wrists stamped. Inside wasn't as bad as I first thought; it looked like a typical male-dominated sports hall. It smelled like it, too. The stench of stale beer, cigarettes, and testosterone clung heavily in the air.

"Let's find some seats." Capri led the way through the rowdy crowd until she spotted two free seats not too far from the front. "Stay here and I'll get us some snacks and shit." She kissed me on the cheek and darted away.

The crowd roared with excitement as the first contestants walked into the cage. I wondered how many fights I'd have to sit through until Tyler's. A small pang of nervous energy settled in my belly, and I couldn't put my finger on why. I ignored it the best I could until Capri came back and juggled two cups of beer, a bag of pretzels, and a bucket of popcorn.

"Get enough food?" I took the beers off her so she could sit.

"Probably not with you around." She threw a piece of popcorn at me.

"Hey." I flinched and spilled a little beer.

Our attention was diverted to the ring where

one fighter had already been knocked out. "That was quick." Capri snorted.

"Have you ever watched Tyler fight?" I glanced down at her.

She nodded and shoved a handful of popcorn in her mouth before chewing for what felt like ages. "He's pretty good. I think he's gone up a weight division, though. You know how big he is." She smirked at me.

"No, I actually don't, if that's what you're referring to." I handed her one of the beers so I could grab some popcorn.

The crowd around us started to clap and scream, and we were all of a sudden the only two seated. We copied those around us and stood to see what was going on.

My eyes caught sight of Tyler in the ring, and my heart jackhammered in my chest. His muscles looked bigger somehow under the harsh lights above. His tattoos shone like warrior paint, and the look of determination on his face fascinated me. I'd only known him as the easy-going one out of the four. He always seemed so fun and carefree. Now, in the ring, he looked lethal. He prowled around the ring like a predator in waiting and bounced on the balls of his feet. His opponent climbed in, and the crowd booed and threw empty beer cups at the side of the ring.

"I guess he's not popular." I glanced at Capri, who was grinning from ear to ear.

"Tyler is hometown favorite." She winked up at me, and I rolled my eyes.

The nervousness edged its way higher up my throat, and I felt like I couldn't breathe just as the bell rang for the start of the fight. I watched in amazement at the lithe movements of both men, their skin covered in a sheen of sweat as they kicked and wrestled. Tyler was slammed into the ground, and I yelped in response. I took a big gulp of the beer I held. The cold liquid slid down my throat but did nothing to extinguish the fire in my belly.

"Holy fuck, did you see that?" Capri shouted over the roar of the crowd, and I nodded.

I took another big mouthful of beer and watched on as the two fighters belted each other. They seemed equally matched as they maneuvered and dodged one another in the ring. Finally, Tyler knocked the other fighter out and I could breathe again. I skulled the rest of the beer to help cool myself down.

"Hey, you okay?" Capri shouted over the roar of the cheering crowd.

"No. Fuck me." I blew out a breath.

Capri chuckled and grabbed my hand. "Let's get out of here. We're all meeting at the Club House. It's tradition." She winked.

"Of course it is." I rolled my eyes at her. The town and its fucking traditions.

We blasted Eminem all the way back to St. Ivy and parked on the deserted road down near the cliffs. The roar of the ocean swirled around us as the wind picked up. The humid salty air had a bite to it, and I shivered from the sudden chill. We climbed through the old wooden fence and made our way past the row of tall palms trees. Foggy mist had settled around the old stone building and made it look like a set from a Tim Burton Halloween special. The faint smells of pot lingered, and I eyed the group of people lazily spread out on the lawn in front of the bonfire. I spotted Maddie with her minions and decided I'd stay the fuck away from her as best I could.

"Want a drink?" Capri headed to the bar inside.

"Why the hell not." I shrugged. I'd already

drunk that disgusting beer at the fights. What was one extra drink?

Capri looked at me then. 'Really?"

"One won't hurt." I smiled and followed her into the Club House.

We both headed to the bar where Frankie was busy mixing drinks for other students.

"Peyton!" she screamed as she turned to face us. "You're here!"

"I am," I answered.

Capri gripped me around the neck and pulled me into her. "And she's drinking."

Frankie nodded, a wicked smirk spreading over her face. "I'm going to make you my signature cocktail. Don't move." She ducked down behind the bar to do who knew what.

As Frankie set about mixing our drinks, I twisted on my seat to take a look around at the others. Some I recognized from school, others I thought looked too old to be St. Ivy students. They lazed around on the aged chesterfields puffing on cigars and drinking whiskey from tumblers. It looked odd, like an old gentleman's club filled with children.

The flicker of the flame torches on the walls reminded me of medieval castles long abandoned. The haze of cigar smoke hung near the ceiling like a veil of poison. The smell made my nose wrinkle, and the remnants of vaulted memories threatened to invade my thoughts. I turned back to the bar to see Frankie place a turquoise-colored drink in front of me and Capri.

"It's coconut flavored. I see you constantly applying that coconut lip balm, so figured you'd like the flavor." She grinned and pushed the drinks further toward us.

The color reminded me of Colton's eyes, the deep aqua with specks of green when he stared down at me ready to destroy me. I swallowed the thought. Fuck. I needed to not think of him. "Thanks." I picked it up and took a sip. "Oh, it's really good." I looked at Capri, who was smiling at me.

"Duh, I made it." Frankie swirled on the spot and returned to mixing drinks.

"So, what's the point of this whole party?" I asked.

"To celebrate Tyler's win." She raised her eyebrows. "And we like to party," she added.

"When did they all get back?" I tried to sound uninterested.

"Dad and Colton stayed longer." She looked at me, answering my unspoken question.

I nodded and sipped my drink.

"Peyton?" The deep voice came across as questioning.

Before I had the time to turn around to see who called my name, Eli deposited himself on the barstool next to me and draped his arm around my shoulder.

"Hey." I offered him a sip of my drink.

"I'm going to find Jasper." With that, Capri quickly disappeared.

"So." Eli grabbed my drink out of my hand and wrapped his lips around the straw, all the while eye-fucking me.

"So." I cleared my throat. I glanced down at my drink in his hand to stop myself from looking into his eyes. It's when I noticed the fresh cuts on his knuckles.

"Want to go sit near the bonfire?" He gave me back my drink and stood.

"I guess." I drank the rest of the sweet coconut cocktail and followed him outside. The party had doubled in the time we had been inside, and I noticed a large group gathered around something.

Eli headed to the bonfire, where there weren't many drunk teenagers. I followed him, but not before I craned my neck to see who everyone was gathered around. I spotted Tyler, flanked by Steele and Hawke, his face battered and swollen still. I quickly turned before any of them spotted me and disappeared into the dark.

"This is better." Eli stopped and glanced at me.

I did admit to myself, that this was much nicer than the rowdy crowd. I relaxed into the warmth. I paused as his eyes drank me in. "So, whose face did you smack around?" I glanced down at his knuckles.

He stiffened at my question. "Just some dick." His smile dazzled in the firelight.

"Right." I narrowed my eyes at him. "Are you in with them?"

"With who?" He moved closer to me so our arms touched.

"Steele and his gang."

Eli burst out laughing. "Steele and his gang. No, I'm not Steele's minion." He ran his hand through his already messy hair.

"Right." I kept my thoughts to myself. I

didn't believe him. I'd seen how they all acted around each other.

Eli leaned into me, his mouth hovering over my ear. "Want to get out of here?"

"No, she fucking doesn't." Steele's voice pulsated through the air as it cock blocked Eli. It hit me in all the wrong ways, fucking yet again.

How did this jerk-off have such an effect on me? "Excuse me?" I turned to stare up at him and his fucking perfect face only, to see both Hawke and Tyler next to him. My eyes scanned Tyler's face. His swollen eye, split lip, and bruises made my stomach lurch. The big dick energy these fuckers emitted had my girly hormones in a confused rage.

Eli had straightened back up but didn't stop touching me. His hand moved to my chin, and he tilted it so I connected my gaze with his. "Don't worry about it. I'll see you around." He winked.

I heard a low growl but didn't know who it came from before Eli walked away.

"You happy, big boy?" I glared up at Steele to be met with a satisfied evil smirk.

"Like you wouldn't fucking believe." They

moved to hover around me.

I couldn't take my eyes off Tyler's face. He looked to be in pain and I wanted to take that pain away. Ugh, I needed to get a hold of myself.

As though he could read my thoughts, Tyler smiled at me. The corner of his mouth barely moved, thanks to the swelling. "It's not as bad as it looks. Besides, I won."

"I know." I sighed, still unable to tear my eyes away from him.

"You came to watch?" His face lit up ever so slightly.

I nodded.

"Aww, Bambi, I'm flattered." He chuckled.

"Why are you all such fucktards all the time?" I huffed and crossed my arms. I wanted to walk away from them, but they had me trapped. The only way out of their cornering was through the bonfire.

"Because we can be," Hawke piped up. He hardly ever spoke to me and I wondered if his dislike for me stemmed from these two.

Tyler stepped closer to me. "Don't deny you don't love it." I wanted to swipe the cocky smirk off his face, but he looked battered and bruised enough.

"I'm not Maddie. I don't put up with all your shit." I balled my fists at my sides.

"Hey, Maddie," Steele called across the yard.

I groaned, and Hawke shot me a look with a twisted meaning. Did I just see him roll his eyes and tighten his jaw? I cocked an eyebrow at him as Maddie approached. Did we have a mutual hatred for Queen Bee? Hawke winked at me as Maddie stood between him and Steele. Her overbearing perfume was so potent that it made me wrinkle my nose.

"What's happening?" She leaned in and kissed Steele on the cheek, her whiny voice annoying as fuck.

I studied them and found their interactions slightly off. Something about how they barely touched each other and how she didn't throw herself at him. Come to think of it, I didn't think I'd seen her actually all over him once. Weird.

Steele interrupted my thoughts. "Peyton here was just telling us how much she wanted to be just like you." Steele's hand snaked its way around her waist, and he held her possessively without taking his eyes off me.

Some irrational jealous monster lurked inside me, and it took all of my self-control not to rip her from his side and tear her face off. My therapist's voice echoed in my head like a broken record, and I managed to control my emotions just enough not to have an outburst. This time. I caught Hawke's intense gaze on me as he studied my reaction. I thought I had kept my cool but from his expression, I wasn't so sure.

"Of course she does. I mean, look at her." Miss Queen Bee looked down her nose at me. A nose I had the urge to break.

I held my tongue and flitted my eyes to Steele. His bemused features stared back at me, hoping to rile me up. But I wasn't going to bite. I took in a deep breath and glanced at Tyler before I broke through the gap between him and Steele and left them to their celebrations. I wasn't in the mood for them.

I made my way back to the Club House and found Frankie still behind the bar making drinks for everyone. I sat on an empty bar stool and watched her, tuning out. I didn't know how long I sat there for, but I hadn't noticed Tyler had parked himself beside me.

"Do you trust me?" he whispered into my ear.

I froze as the words he just spoke came back to haunt me. "Not really." I shook my head and tried not to focus on the memories of my past and how that deranged fucker said those exact words to me.

"Bad luck, then." He gripped my hand in his and pulled me off the bar stool and back toward the darkened hallway.

"That's a fucking bad idea, Tyler." Frankie's voice faded into the background.

I didn't care at this point. I needed a distraction from my thoughts and the memories about to invade my headspace. I was also keen to get far away from Steele and his preppy girlfriend before my jealousy did something we would both regret.

I watched as Tyler pressed his silver skull ring to the keypad, and the door slid across to reveal a set of stairs that led to a pit of darkness.

CHAPTER SIXTEEN

Peyton

The stale air had a hint of cedar and remnants of expensive cigars, and the scents became stronger the further we descended. I gripped Tyler's hand as he led me down a never-ending set of wooden stairs. Our footsteps echoed around us, and I didn't know how the fuck Tyler knew where he was going because I couldn't see shit. It was pitch black and disorientating.

"Ready?" Tyler announced as he switched the dim lights on to reveal a cold room with walls made of mismatched gray stones.

I eyed the place with caution. "Why are we down here?" My heart started to panic and beat erratically in my chest. Two chestnut-colored chesterfields were placed in the center of the room facing each other with an enormous golden globe-looking thing between them propped up on a marble stand. Only it wasn't a globe, it was a gold skull, the same as all their rings. What the fuck was this place?

Tyler turned around to face me. He stood eye to eye with me, as I'd stopped on the second last step. "Seeking revenge." Tyler's throat bobbed as he swallowed, and a feral grin revealed his perfect teeth.

"What revenge?" I tilted my head and wondered what the hell he was talking about. His face had started to color, purple bruises and red splotches decorated him, and the swelling of his eye seemed to have stopped.

I heard the quiet footsteps as they descend the stairs, and my stomach bottomed out. This wasn't happening. My eyes darted around the room to find another escape. A lone door sat to the far right and it was bolted shut. Fuck. These fuckers were going to give me what they promised from the very beginning.

"Ready to play, little Bambi?" Steele brushed past me, headed to the bolted door, and left a trail of cigarette smoke behind him. He was dressed in his usual jeans and an extra tight black t-shirt that showed off his mouthwatering muscles.

"Lock and load baby," Hawke called from behind me, and I heard the door at the top of the stairs thud.

"Let's go." Tyler managed a half wink with his battered eye.

"Fuck off. I'm not going in there with you three." I stepped back into Hawke's muscled stomach, and the sudden feeling of being trapped made me nauseous. His arm circled me, the pressure was strangely calming and helped keep the panic attack at bay.

Steele paused as my words rang in the otherwise silent room. He twisted to glare at me and cracked his neck. His switchblade flicked in his hands, and he dragged in a lungful of his cigarette. He closed the distance between us in a split second and shoved Tyler out of his way.

I stood my ground. Even though the closeness of all three of them had my panties soaked, I wasn't about to surrender to their vicious charms.

Steele blew smoke in my face as he took the cigarette from between his luscious lips. I was drawn into the movements of his mouth as his tongue darted out and wet the spot where the cigarette had just been. "Don't pretend you don't get off on us fucking around with you." His voice made me quiver.

I swallowed as his eyes slid to my mouth, and his sinister thoughts were written all over his face. He dragged in another lungful of cigarette and blew the smoke out in circles. My brain focused on his tongue and all the dirty things I wanted him to do to me.

"We know it gets you wet and thirsty for the cock. It's been so fucking obvious from the very beginning. You act all prissy and proper, thinking your pussy is too good for us. We could hold you down right here and you'd beg us for more. But that's too easy. I want you fucking conflicted. I want you to be begging for it and at the same time hating yourself for giving in. I want your mind to crack. I want to fucking own you, mind, body, and soul. As I promised, Peyton, I will fucking break you. But tonight is not that night."

He flicked the switchblade in my face and stormed back to the bolted door.

His words sat heavy in the air, and neither Tyler or Hawke said a word to me. Hawke's arm fell away as he nudged me from behind and made me step further into the room. "It's not what you're thinking," he whispered.

I twisted and glanced up at him. His slicked-back hair and broody dark chocolate eyes greeted me. His lips curved and met me with a low grunt as he bumped me again. For some strange reason, I trusted his word and moved to stand behind Steele as he unlocked the door.

The smell of bleach nearly knocked me for six. "Holy fuck, that's so strong." I placed my hand over my nose and mouth and allowed Hawke to herd me in after Tyler and Steele.

"Look who we have here." Tyler pulled a string and a fluorescent light nearly blinded me.

A gasp escaped my lips as my eyes connected with a guy tied to a chair with a gag in his mouth. "What the fuck?" I stepped back and tried to leave. Hawke's firm grip held me in place.

The guy's eyes grew wild with fear when they landed on me, and he jerked around and nearly tipped himself over. Tyler moved to stand behind the guy and gripped his shoulders to hold him still.

"Take a good look at this fucker's eyes, Peyton. Do you remember him?" Steele singed the guy's cheek with his cigarette and then put it out and flicked it on the floor.

My heart hammered in my chest, and I wanted to turn around and get the fuck out, but a dormant part of me fought to escape from the dark depths within. The depths of my brain that I fought so hard to keep hidden. I stepped forward and studied the guy's red-rimmed eyes. He looked as though he had been down here for a few days, His clothes were covered in urine and feces stains, but there was no evidence of it on the floors.

Tyler gripped the guy's hair and jerked his head back for me to get a better look. "I don't know who he is," I whispered and stepped back away from him.

Steele flicked his wrist to cut the gag from the guy's mouth.

"I'm not fucking talking," the guy yelled, trying to jerk his head out of Tyler's grip.

Steele backhanded the guy, and a flow of crimson blood trickled down the guy's cheek. "I'm not a patient man." Steele leaned down so he was face to face with the guy. "Tell her who fucking ordered her a spiked drink."

I froze, and it all came back to me. His fucking eyes. It was the fucker at the front door from the secret party. All thoughts, emotions, and senses ceased in me then. I charged for him and sent my fist into his face. The sting in my knuckles barely registered as I pummeled into his face over and over until firm arms gripped me around my waist and hauled me away. My eyes were wild with fury when I was placed back on my feet.

"Slow down, psycho, we still need him to be able to talk," Hawke told me.

Steele looked at me with admiration. "Fuck yes, Bambi. Who knew you had that hiding inside you?" He grinned like a crazy person and held up his blade toward me. "Want to slice him?"

I looked at the knife longingly for a second before I shook my head as the adrenaline slowly started to dissolve and the pounding pain in my fist reminded me of what I just did. I glanced at the guy's face, covered in fresh blood, as it hung to the side.

Tyler slapped the guy's cheek to wake him up enough to talk. He stirred, but the vacant look in his eyes told me he had given up and nothing these guys could do would make him talk. I knew that haunted look. I had witnessed it many times, and the memories sent a bone-chilling shiver over my skin.

Steele squatted down in front of the guy and traced his blade along his thigh. Without warning, he plunged the blade into the guy's leg and left it there. The guy roared in agony as the blood started to seep out. "There you are. I'll ask you again. Do you want to tell this lovely young lady who ordered her a spiked drink?" Steele watched as the guy blew snot bubbles out of his nose as he tried to control his whimpers.

The guy's eyes locked onto mine and he let out a feral growl. "Fuck her," he spat in Steele's face.

"Well then." Steele laughed and the sound was truly nightmarish. He stood and wiped the bloody spit off him with his shirt. I caught a glimpse of his muscled stomach, and my saliva dried up in my mouth. I was truly fucking broken at this point.

"Come on, man. I'm in no mood to get messy tonight. Think you could just tell us and save us all the clean-up?" Steele tried to bargain, the look of a practiced killer hardened his features.

They guy surveyed the three and his eyes landed on me. "I'll pay you. How much do you want?"

Steele circled him, his footsteps slow and deliberate. "Do we look like we need money, dipshit?"

The guy's eyes closed for a moment as he thought over his next words. "Just kill me."

A sick sense of satisfaction burrowed into me at his surrender.

The guy opened his eyes and glared at me again. "All I'll say is, watch your fucking back, Blue." He threatened.

A buzzing sound filled my ears, and my head felt like it was about to explode. Was this what it felt like to have a stroke? I felt numb, and my vision started to fade. Small speckles danced around the edges of my eyes until they all joined up in the middle and I couldn't see. I couldn't hear over the loud buzzing, and I couldn't remember where I was. All I knew was that I needed to escape. I needed to run, to feel the cool air on my face before I passed out.

I came to with Tyler and Hawke hovered over me. "What happened?" I sat up and realized I was upstairs in the main Club House area.

Tyler sat on the chesterfield next to me. "I think you had some sort of panic attack."

"Where's Steele?" I glanced around the room and didn't see him amongst the party guests.

"Taking care of business." Hawke coughed.

I knew not to speak of what was done down there. Of the pure white room with tiled walls and floors that stunk of bleach. Of the long drain built adjacent to the furthest wall. Of the stainless-steel sink with the hose attached to it. Or of the hooks on the ceiling and the chains hanging from them. I knew what that room was. I knew what they did in there. The only thing I didn't know was why.

Tyler watched me carefully. "We're taking you home."

"Where's Capri?" I looked at the now empty bar area.

"We told her we'd take you home. She's with Jasper," Hawke explained. I was glad she was with Jasper.

I stood slowly as my legs still wobbled and followed the two of them out of the Club House and away from Steele. I didn't look back as the two guys led me to their car. The party was still in full swing, and I caught the obvious scowl thrown my way from Maddie. She stood with her besties and eye-rolled me as we walked past to get to the guys' cars.

"As if Mr. Knight wasn't enough. Now you're going to fuck them too." She flipped me the finger, and I smiled at her. Good. Let her think I was going home with Tyler and Hawke. Let her jealous ass stew on that all night.

We traipsed through the field and made it to the deserted road to where a handful of cars remained. I didn't spot Capri's, and I hoped she definitely was with Jasper. Tyler stopped at his matte black G Wagon with its obnoxiously big tires. "Of course this is yours." I half-smiled. I looked up at the door and wondered how the fuck I was going to climb into it; there were no steps.

Tyler winked at me and headed over to the driver's side.

"Need a boost?" Hawke pulled the passenger door open just as the thing roared to life.

Before I could decline his offer, he bent down and gripped me around the hips, then lifted me so I could get my leg up on the floor of the cabin. His large hand landed on my ass as he pushed me, causing me to tumble in. Of course, the bastard would take the perfect opportunity to grip my ass. I righted myself and scooted over on the seat to make room.

Hawke climbed in and winked at me. I liked this less serious and broody version of him. I had no idea why he was in such a good mood or why they were all being so chivalrous to me, but I hoped it lasted a while longer.

"We good?" Tyler revved the engine.

I glanced around the front seats of the G Wagon and didn't understand why I couldn't have just sat in the back seat. With the two guys in here, there was hardly any room. They were both so big and I wondered if they often drove girls home together. I shook my head to get that thought out of it and concentrated on the radio.

"We good," Hawke answered, pulling his phone out.

The ride back home was bumpy through the wooded area and the deserted road, but once we hit the main road that ran adjacent to the beach, we were home in no time. There was no need for small talk, which I was eternally grateful for because Hawke had connected his phone and turned the music up to full volume.

Tyler turned into the driveway and rolled up to the front of the house, where I spotted Colton as he casually leaned against the railing on the front porch. *Fuck.*

CHAPTER SEVENTEEN

Peytan

"Bossman looks pissy." Tyler chuckled. "Should we give him something to be pissy about?" He breathed against my neck, and I jerked away from him into Hawke.

"I like pissing him off." Hawke circled his arm around my waist and pulled me onto his lap, nuzzling into my neck and sending traitorous heat to places it had no right to go.

"Stop it." I tried to wriggle out of his grip as I opened the door and froze. Holy shit it was fucking high up here. My gaze connected with Colton's menacing glare.

"Need me to come to help you down, Bambi?" Tyler teased.

I watched Colton stride to the G Wagon and wait at my open door. "Pass her down"

Pass her down. It irritated me more than it should have. But I had no time to argue when Hawke gripped my waist and practically threw me at Colton. "Fucking asshole," I hissed as I smashed into Colton's very capable arms.

I heard the guys' roar of laughter before Hawke closed the door and they drove off.

Colton had a death grip on me at first before he eased up and I slid down his chest. "Where the fuck were you?" His voice vibrated through his chest and against me.

"None of your fucking business."

His grip on me tightened possessively. "Is that so?"

I pressed my palms against his firm chest and tried to distance myself from him. I was afraid to be this close to him, afraid of what I'd let myself do with him. The rush of adrenaline returned, this time it was from the excitement of being consumed by him again,

"Let me go, Colton." My eyes caught his, and I struggled in his grip to prove I wasn't the same as the other students he fucked and tossed aside.

The curve of his mouth twisted up, and he ran the tongue ring against his lip. "Where were you tonight, Murdoch?" he gritted out.

I hated when he called me that. "I watched Tyler's fight and then went to the Club House with Capri. You know, I had an eventful night. Steele is chopping up some wanker as we speak." I watched him carefully to see his response.

He didn't even flinch. He let go of my waist, gripped my wrist in his fingers, and dragged me into the house. He pulled me into the darkened formal living room and slammed me against the wall. His hands gripped my shoulders, and he pushed me to my knees. As much as I tried to fight against him, his strength overpowered me. I dropped to the floor, and my knees hit the hard wooden floors with a thud. The pain almost made me cry out, but I was too distracted by the swift motion of his hands. He had his zipper undone and his cock pressed against my mouth within seconds.

"Open your fucking mouth," he snarled

through clenched teeth.

"Someone will," I started bitterly before I was rendered speechless by the forced intrusion of his hard cock. It hit the back of my throat as he slammed it in my mouth, and I gagged. Tears threatened my eyes as he moved out of my mouth to let me breathe. I hated myself at that moment. I hated my traitorous body that came alive at the thrill and the power of bringing this man undone.

His hands gripped the sides of my head as he continued his movements. I was equally mortified that someone could walk past and find us like this and also so fucking wet at the thought of being caught.

"Next time you open your fucking mouth about what goes on in the Brotherhood, I will not be this forgiving." He held my head firm as he fucked my mouth.

I gripped his legs as his movements increased in speed. My head was wedged against the wall, and the head of his dick hit the back of my throat with each thrust

He groaned as his release shot down my throat and he gave one last jerk into my mouth before he gripped the base of his dick and pulled out of my mouth. He wiped the leftover cum over my chin with his fingers. He didn't speak, and he didn't even look at me before he zipped his pants back up and left me in the dark, on my knees, like a fucking obedient idiot.

I sat there for a few moments and gathered myself together. He left me needy and wanting release. His raw power and dominance had my pussy humming for more. I wiped my chin on the back of my hand and stood up. I then headed to the kitchen and found my mom at the bench working on her laptop.

"Honey, you're home early." She glanced up at me and kept her thoughts to herself.

I must have looked like a mess. I ran my hands through my hair and tried to pat it down as best I could. I could still feel the dull ache in my knees as I moved around the kitchen. "It was getting boring, so some friends dropped me home." I opened the fridge and stared into it.

"Is Capri still there?" Mom asked.

I nodded. "She's with Jasper." Even though Capri kept her boyfriend from her dad, Mom knew all about the amazing Jasper. Why did I pine after assholes? Ugh.

"That boy is such a sweetheart." I could hear the smile in Mom's voice.

I grabbed the strawberry milk out and poured myself a glass while I watched my mom work. My thoughts flicked to Colton, and I wondered what he was doing right now. Where had he stormed off to?

"Are you okay, honey?" Mom looked at me with concern.

"I had two drinks and I feel queasy," I confessed.

Mom grinned at me. "Take some Tylenol and a glass of water and go to bed."

"You're not going to get angry?" I gave her a dumbfounded look.

She laughed. "No, I'm happy to see you being a normal teenager for once." She closed her laptop and came around to where I stood. "I love you, my girl." She wrapped her arms around me and pulled me into her.

"I love you too, Mom." I gripped her back. It used to be so hard for me to allow someone to show me affection, but I'd worked through that, and nothing compared to my mom's hugs. Fuck, I loved her.

She let go of me and grabbed her laptop. "I'm going to bed."

"Did you wait up for me to get home?" My heart ended up in my throat. Fuck. What if she heard Colton earlier?

"Always." She smiled at me before she headed upstairs to her master suite.

I wanted to hurl at the thought of my mom hearing us.

I placed the milk back in the fridge and rinsed my glass before I scrambled upstairs. I headed straight for my balcony and saw that his lights were on and a small part of me, okay, the fucking green-eyed jealous monster part of me, was glad he was here and not at someone's place.

I wandered back inside and ran a bath to soak away my troubles. I popped in a coconut bath bomb and waited for it to fizz out before I climbed in and sunk under the water to wet my hair. My thoughts, as usual, concentrated on the bad shit. My brain kept going back to the one word Colton said. The Brotherhood. What the fuck did he mean when he said that? I also tried not to dwell on the fact that someone from my past knew I was here. Knew where to find me and knew they called me Blue. Who the hell was he, and who the fuck sent him? I was very glad that he'd been dealt with, and I'd hoped for his sake that Steele had carried out whatever he did, relatively quickly. I needed to get to the bottom of this, and if that meant contacting Dylan again, then I'd have to face the consequences. I wouldn't allow them near my mom and near the life she had set up for us away from there.

I climbed out of the bath once the water cooled, wrapped myself in my fluffy white bathrobe, climbed into bed, and turned on some music. I couldn't sleep in silence. It gave me anxiety. I needed the noise to distract me from my thoughts. I fell asleep as I listened to Eminem on repeat.

It was early Monday morning when I woke to the sound of the waves as they crashed against the shore. I climbed out of bed and threw on a pair of denim shorts and a hoodie, then made my way to the beach. I passed the pool house, but it was closed up and dark inside, and my heart fluttered stupidly as I left it behind me.

The sand was cool and tickled my toes as my feet padded along the dunes down to the surf. The salty ocean breeze swirled around me and tossed my long hair into my face. I gathered it and twisted it up into a messy bun to stop any further knots. I spotted surfers in the distance and wondered if one was Tyler. Without even thinking, I found myself drawn to them and headed to the area in front of his house.

I sat on the sand and watched the surfers as they caught wave after wave and bobbed on their boards out past the breakers. How calming and soothing it must be out there, with nothing but you and the ocean and her sounds and scents.

I didn't know how long I'd been sitting in the same spot, but the three guys out there were headed to shore and rose out of the water like three kings of the sea. I watched them as they placed their boards on the wet sand just out of reach of the sea and unzipped their wetsuits to let them hang on their hips.

I stood and was about to head back home when a familiar deep voice called out to me.

"Peyton, wait," Tyler shouted, jogging up towards me. He stopped at the bottom of the sand dunes and shook the water out of his hair. My eyes caught the muscles on his stomach as he moved, and I noticed the deep purple bruises that decorated his torso.

"They look worse than they feel." His lopsided grin made me smile.

"Glad to hear it."

I watched as Hawke and Steele wandered up to stand beside Tyler and wedged their boards upright into the sand. My eyes feasted over their tanned skin, covered in delicious tattoos and piercings. I spotted the same tattoo on all of them, a barely visible white skull with vines circling it. Their trademark? Their gang sign? Their Brotherhood? I had no clue what they were all a part of, but I doubted it was legal.

"You'll be happy to know that the fucker last night suffered a terrible overdose. It took ages for him to fucking die. The frothing of the mouth was the best part." Steele's eyes drank me in as he revealed this.

I sucked in a breath.

"Eye for an eye, Bambi." Hawke winked.

I swallowed the nerves that suddenly crept

up, I needed to stop looking at the three of them. The more I gawked at their deliciousness, the more I accepted their depraved ways. "I've got to go get ready for school." I turned on the spot and started for our house.

"See you in class." Steele's voice carried in the wind and hit me with its usual level of sinfulness.

I managed to pry Capri from her bed and helped her get ready for school. She'd got in sometime early this morning after spending the night with Jasper, so I dosed her up on caffeine and drove us to school.

I spotted Tyler's monster G Wagon parked over two car spots and smiled inwardly. Of course he would think it was his god given right to take up two parks. *Typical asshole,* I thought to myself in an adoring manner.

I settled Capri into her first class and made sure Katie looked after her. Then I headed to the teacher faculty building to hand in my history assignment. It wasn't due until next week, but I wanted to get it out of the way and out of my mind so I could focus on my other end-of-term assessments. I couldn't believe that it was nearly the end of term. How had it flown by so fast? And what an eventful term it had been. I hoped it didn't set the precedent for the rest of the year, or I feared I wouldn't survive.

I rounded the corner and headed down the long hall toward the teacher's office when I happened to pass his. As much as I tried to stop myself from glancing into his office, I mean, he had the goddamned door open. So, any normal human being with a heartbeat would naturally take a look. I wish I'd fucking hadn't.

My heart caught in my throat when I saw her in there with him. Colton stood behind his desk, arms crossed, as she leaned onto the desk and stuck her tits in his face.

Anger and hurt circled within me as I stood there a moment too long. They both turned to look at me, Colton's face disguised in anger and her face plastered in what one would call cocky satisfaction. I glared at her as her glee for being caught in his room shone like a lighthouse beacon in a rough storm. Only, what I felt brew inside me was much worse than any storm these two had ever encountered.

At that moment, without looking at him again, I took off. My rage burned through my veins and felt like hot lava. I could barely see where I was going thanks to the tears that threatened to spill over. I chided myself for crying over someone who wasn't even mine. Someone who could never be mine, be that because of him being my teacher or stepbrother. I decided right there that I would never cry over him, or any male, again.

I found a darkened room and slammed the door shut until I got myself and my shit together. I had no right to feel this way. He simply fucked me once and that was it. I was at a constant war with myself in my head. It didn't matter how I felt when I was with him, or how he made me feel whole again. How I felt alive and a little closer to the old me, the Peyton from the past before the trauma. How he didn't treat me like I was a fragile little girl who needed protecting. He had been cruel and almost violent with his words and actions and he never promised anything.

I should never have let myself feel. Fucking girly feelings.

The room I'd hidden in, I discovered, was the stationery storeroom, and I hoped to fucking hell no teacher needed supplies this morning. I heard hurried footsteps, and I froze when they stopped outside the door. Great. I watched the door slowly open as my heart pounded against my chest to the point of pain. Colton's acidic glare slammed against me. He looked pissed. He always looked pissed.

He stormed into the small room and slammed the door behind him. "What the fuck was that about?" He pressed me against the shelves of paper and pens. My chest tightened and I stared up at him like a deer in headlights. If I let words come out of my mouth, I knew I'd regret them, so I kept quiet.

"Answer me." His eyes darted from mine to my lips and back. He could taste the jealousy on me.

"It was nothing." I wanted to hit him. If he was so stupid to not know what the fuck my problem was, then he could be kept in the dark about it.

His nostrils flared. "Didn't look like nothing."

I laughed. I fucking laughed in his face.

"You don't say."

His eyebrows furrowed, and he narrowed his eyes at me. "Nothing was going on. I've never even touched the fucking girl," he snarled.

"I don't care who you fuck, Colton," I spat at him, but the tone of my voice didn't match the way I felt. The storm that I'd threatened a few moments ago started to be replaced by a hurricane of raw emotion.

He didn't buy it.

He watched me intently. Our breaths fell in time with each other, both heavy with lust and desire and illicit need. My heart pounded in my chest as his wicked mouth found mine. His hands roamed my bare thighs as he lifted my school skirt and gripped my ass. He hoisted me up so I could wrap my legs around his hips.

Colton pulled away and stared into my eyes. "You drive me fucking crazy, Murdoch," he said before he rested his forehead against mine, his breathing ragged and erratic.

I felt him shift, and I tightened my arms around his neck. With one hand still on my ass, he unzipped his pants and slid my panties aside. He stared into my eyes for a moment, as if to ask for permission. As if he needed this as much as I did. I kissed him deeply and explored his tongue ring. This was enough for him to understand I wanted this too. That I needed it as much as he did.

He slipped his cock inside me, slowly and deliberately, and ensured I was filled with him before he gazed into my eyes again. This felt different from before. This felt raw and real. Like he was exposing his vulnerable side to me. Gone was the vicious and aggressive Colton, and in his place was this man before me. His slow thrusts picked up rhythm and a low moan escaped my trembling lips.

"Colton, we're going to get caught." I bit my lower lip as my orgasm teased me.

"Shh, Murdoch." He clamped down on my shoulder and then flicked his tongue ring over the sting.

I closed my eyes as his thrusts became feral in both nature and intensity. My back was going to be bruised from the repetitive movements and the constant grazing of the shelves behind me. I didn't care. I barely registered the pain from the sharp edges. Licks of insatiable hunger tore at my mind as he unleashed his delicious assault on my pussy. "I'm going to come," I breathed through clenched teeth as I came undone and my orgasm threatened to make me scream.

"Scream for me." He buried his face in my neck and squeezed my ass cheeks before he suddenly pulled out and dropped me to my feet. A strangled groan vibrated against me as he fumbled with the shelves until his hand landed on what he was looking for.

The reason for his sudden movement away from me became apparent when I watched him milk his cock and shoot his release into a small plastic cup. His chest heaved as he came down from his high, like a wild beast. It was primal and animalistic the way he glanced at me and his eyes raked over my disheveled uniform.

He stepped into me again and pressed the edge of the cup to my lips. "Swallow for me." His voice was velvety smooth and washed over me like silk. His request was fucking depraved and vile, but I couldn't say no. Something inside me wanted to match him sin for sin, so I let him pour his release into my mouth and I swallowed it whole.

He stared down at me, his corrupt ways displayed on his features once again, and I was afraid the Colton from moments ago was gone. I glanced behind him and noticed the narrow crack of light from the door. "Didn't you close the door properly? Fuck, Colton." I pushed him away from me and fixed my panties back in place.

He chuckled and shook his head slowly from side to side. "You stress too much." He grabbed my hand and pulled me into his chest. "Don't worry; you're the only one I'm fucking." His eyes grew dark as the words left his mouth.

I didn't know whether that was a lie or not. All I knew was this time around was different. He looked at me like he didn't know if he wanted to destroy me or devour me. Colton's conflicted glare sent heat through my body, and I needed to distance myself from him. Especially as we were on school grounds. Fuck. He was going to get me expelled. He seemed to come to the same conclusion and with that, he turned and exited the stationary supply room without closing the door after him.

CHAPTER EIGHTEEN

Peyton

Friday afternoon had finally rolled around. I'd wandered down to the beach after school, and found myself gazing at the ocean as the afternoon sun showered the sea in orange and golden rays. I hadn't seen Colton again after the stationery storeroom session the other morning. I didn't know if he was avoiding me or had business to attend to, as usual. He seemed to always have time off from work.

The days all melded together and were otherwise drama free, apart from Maddie. I'd only been subjected to the Queen Bee's glares and smirks every damn lunch break as she had whispered dumb shit to her friends, which now included Stass, to make them stare at me and laugh.

"You look deep in thought." Tyler placed his surfboard on the sand and sat down next to me.

I picked up a broken shell and twirled it in my fingertips. "You're observant."

"Only when it comes to you." He nudged my arm.

My gaze slid to his and with the way he eyed me, I wasn't sure if he meant that as a joke or he was being serious.

"Don't look so worried." He laughed and jumped up to hold his hand out for me.

I eyed him speculatively. "What?"

"I'm teaching you to surf. No is not an answer I'm going to accept. So, you either come willingly, or I'll carry you in." He grinned at me, and the mischievous glee in his face made my insides squirm, in a good way.

I glanced down at my clothes in the hopes he'd retract his offer. "I'm not really dressed for surfing."

"It doesn't require a dress code, Bambi." He

tilted his head.

"No, I can't," I protested.

"Can't or won't?"

I shook my head. "I don't think this is such a good idea."

"I'll give you three seconds." He grabbed his board and waited.

"Fine. If you drown me, I'm going to kill you." I stood up and pulled off my top. Thank goodness I was wearing a black sports bra. I kept my denim shorts on, there was no way in hell I was going surfing in my panties.

Tyler gazed at me, his desire was written all over his face. "How will you kill me once you're already dead?" He chuckled as he headed for the surf.

Those words should have bothered me, but they didn't, and I followed him to the edge of the water. My heart beat steadily as the exhilaration of being out there with nothing but the ocean slowly built within me.

"You coming?" Tyler called behind him, he was waist-deep in the water with the surfboard ready and waiting.

I waded in until I reached him, only the water was up to my ribs, and I realized how much taller he was.

"Hop on." He waggled his eyebrows.

"Is that your way of flirting?" I placed my hands on the board and tried to hoist myself up. It was fucking difficult. I barely moved out of the water as the surfboard moved under my weight. A big wave crashed into us and I held my breath as it went over me. I resurfaced to see Tyler a few feet away, paddling back toward me.

"Grab my arm." He held his hand out to me, and I took it. Without any effort, he hauled me onto his back so I was laying firmly against him. "Hold on, Bambi." He positioned us so we floated over the next wave and began paddling out further.

I held onto his shoulders as his strong arms paddled us out past the breakers. It was serenely quiet out this far. Neither of us talked for a few moments, and we both lay there and took in the peacefulness. The noise of the crashing waves sounded muted and was overshadowed by my racing heart.

"You're not scared of sharks are you?" Tyler slid us both off the board and I scrambled to hold on to him.

"Why the fuck would you say that?" I slapped his arm.

He threw his head back and roared with laughter. "I never thought I'd see the day where you were scared. You should see your face." He gripped me around the waist and pulled me into him. "I won't let the big bad sharks get you."

It felt like there was a double edge to his words. A hidden meaning that I was yet to work out. "Gee, thanks."

"Here, give me your ankle." He reached down and tried to grab my foot.

I lifted my leg for him. "Why?"

"So I can strap the board to you. Just in case we get separated, you'll have something to cling on to apart from me." He grinned, as he fastened the Velcro strap around my ankle.

"Oh, okay." I let him move me so I had my back to his chest and I placed both my palms on the board.

"Ready, I'll lift you up, but I need you to try position yourself onto the board." He gripped my waist and I felt his thumbs rub circles on my lower back.

"Okay." I tried not to think of how deep the

water was out here or what lurked underneath.

Tyler hoisted me out of the water and I threw myself as best I could onto the surfboard. I must have looked like a fucking seal flapping about on my stomach, but I managed to get myself turned to face the right way on the board. I grinned like I'd just won first place in a math competition. My shorts were heavy as the water slowly drained from the thick fabric. "Next time we try this, I'm wearing more appropriate clothing."

"So, there will be a next time?" Tyler bobbed in the water next to me.

I looked at him as I adjusted myself on the board. "You know what I mean." His mischievous grin was back and its effect on me had me second-guessing myself.

"Still, you said next time. I'm holding you to that." He placed his hand on my waist and pushed me so I was more in the middle of the board. "Sit up and straddle the board." He ordered.

I did as he said, and managed to not fall off, as I moved myself to be perfectly in the middle of the board. My lower legs dangled into the cool ocean and settled my nerves. The sun's blaze slowly faded and her warmth fast disappeared. I fell instantly in love with the feeling of being out here, with nothing but the sounds of seagulls and the sharp noise of the wind. It was enchanting and I understood why these guys spent hours out here, alone, with nothing but the ocean as company.

Tyler ducked under the water and rose back up looking like a sea god. The remnants of the sun glittered the beads of water as they trickled over his face and landed back in the sea. His face was marked from his fight, but it did not detract from his sex appeal. And he fucking knew it. He caught me checking him out, but he didn't tease me about it.

"Your lips are turning blue. Are you cold?" His eyes stayed focused on my mouth.

"Just a little, but I don't mind." I shrugged, and ran my fingertips through the water.

"Come on, I'll take us back in. Next time, we'll come out earlier. Scoot forward." He pushed on my ass, so I would move forward quicker.

I shuffled forward the best I could, and the next thing I knew the board tipped as Tyler slid on. I nearly fell back into the water, but he caught me around the waist and held me against his shoulder. "You need to warn a girl next time you decide to mount the board."

He chuckled at my choice of words. "Lay on your stomach and scoot backward."

"Excuse me?" I twisted to look at his wide grin.

"If we're going to go back to shore, you need to lay down." He raised his eyebrows as though I was dumb for not knowing that.

"You could have said that in the first place," I huffed, and awkwardly lay down, very aware that my ass was in his face.

"What did you think I was insinuating, Bambi?" I felt his warm breath against my legs, and it sent shivers over my body.

"Don't even start with me, Tyler," I growled.

His cold hands gripped both my thighs and he hauled me closer to him, so his chest pressed against my ass. "You're going to have to help me paddle back in." He started to move his hands through the water and I copied his movements. "When we're about to ride a wave in, make sure you hold on to the board, okay."

"Okay." I had no idea what I was doing, but

this was the most fun I'd had in a long time and I hoped we'd repeat it someday soon.

We paddled between each wave, not that my efforts did anything, but I felt like I was at least helping a little. Each propulsion forward from a large wave made my stomach end up in my throat. I likened it to riding a rollercoaster. The feeling of being free washed over me, and I found myself smiling, and thinking about nothing but the ocean.

As we neared the beach, I spotted two figures on the shoreline, highlighted by the setting sun. They stood with spread legs and folded arms over their muscled chests. I knew it was Hawke and Steele. I would know it was them, even if we'd been further out and they were two tiny stick figures in the distance.

I distracted myself from them by watching the muscles move in Tyler's arms. He paddled and positioned us to catch the waves in until we were close enough to touch the sea floor. "Time to dismount." Tyler slid off the board, reached up to grip my waist and pull me off.

I didn't want to go back ashore. I wanted to stay in the calm ocean until the sun had disappeared over the horizon and took my thoughts with it. I waded through the water with a bit of difficulty. Once we emerged from the water, I headed to where I'd left my t-shirt.

Exactly where Hawke and Steele stood.

Steele watched me as I struggled to pull my t-shirt back on. "Do you know the statistics of people drowning in the ocean?"

"I'm sure you'll tell me." I purposely continued to not look at him.

"It's the third highest cause of death in the world."

I looked at him then, and waited for him to continue with his fact giving. He didn't elaborate, he simply stared at me. "I don't suppose you'd have any input in that statistic?" I accused.

"Nope, that's Tyler's department. I like to slice and dice." His eyes flitted to Tyler, and back. If I hadn't been staring at him, I would have missed it entirely.

"Right." I nodded.

"Hey, dude. Don't give out my secrets." Tyler joked, and pushed Steele in the arm.

My teeth started to chatter as the wind picked up and the sun dipped behind the horizon. I suddenly felt the need to flee, and started to head back toward home when Hawke's voice stopped me in my tracks.

"Are you coming over to start our English assignment?"

Fuck. The one assignment I had been avoiding like the plague. The reason was, I didn't want to be stuck alone with Hawke, all afternoon. Fucking Colton had to be a dick and partner us up when everyone else had got to pick their assignment partners. "I'll just do it all and you can take credit." I waved my hand above me and kept my path.

"No fucking way. I need these marks as much as you." Hawke appeared at my side. I was shocked at how fast he had closed the distance between us.

I stopped walking and turned to look up at him. His deep brown eyes studied me as he waited for my answer. "Fine. I'll go get changed and I'll meet you at your place in ten," I huffed, and stormed off.

This was not how I pictured my Friday night playing out. I had planned to wash my hair, put on a facemask, and watch re-runs of Gilmore Girls with my mom and Capri.

I didn't bother brushing my hair or making

any effort to look half-presentable. I threw on a pair of old sweat pants, with a huge hole in the knee, and a tight black long-sleeve top. I was all about comfort levels if I had to endure spending time with Hawke. I chucked my knotty hair into a messy top bun, grabbed my bag, and headed down to the beach.

The sun had set, and the last glow of its rays set the sky on fire. Clouds of crimson and burnt orange decorated the far horizon, turning the ocean into a deep-hued charcoal blue. I breathed in the salty scent of the sea spray as the angry waves crashed against the shore. The cold sand beneath my toes and the cool ocean air made my skin break out in goosebumps. I hadn't realized how cold it had become or I would have grabbed my hoodie.

I hesitated at the bottom of the dunes that sat outside of Hawke's palatial estate and hoped his parents weren't home. Why had I agreed to this? I squared my shoulders and climbed up the dunes to let myself in through his gate. I eyed the pool house as I passed and wondered if anyone lived in there. I found myself at one of many entrances under the large wrap-around veranda, confused as to which one to knock on. I didn't need to worry because as I stood outside, Hawke waltzed up to the large glass door I was outside of, in nothing but a towel wrapped low around his hips.

I swallowed hard as he opened the door and grinned at me. His hair was still wet and rivulets of water beaded over his muscled chest, down his six-pack, and disappeared into the towel. I spotted the same number 5 tattoo just above his dick and wondered if it meant something.

"Don't just stand there, come inside." He stepped aside, so I could pass.

My eyes snapped to his as I walked into his house, and I turned on the spot to watch him close the door. "So, where are we doing this?" I tried not to stare at his tattoos that were painted haphazardly all across his front and back. There was no rhyme or reason for their placements that I could see.

"If that isn't an innuendo if I've ever heard of one." He waggled his eyebrows.

"Oh my god, seriously. If you're going to be like this all night, I'm going home now and you can explain to Colton why you didn't contribute." I crossed my arms in frustration. I didn't take schoolwork lightly. I studied hard and I expected to get top marks so I had options for college.

"Lighten up," he scoffed, and strode past me. "Are you coming?" he called, as he disappeared around the corner.

I scurried after him and followed his huge muscled frame through the massive kitchen, past the countless hallways and the sunken den. Then up a set of grand stairs until he stopped outside a closed door. I halted my steps and watched him as he turned to me, a smug grin turned up the corner of his lips, and I suddenly worked out we were outside of his room. "Shouldn't we work in the kitchen or something?" I turned and looked back down the long hallway.

"Are you scared?" he chuckled before he opened the door and disappeared in.

I looked at the ceiling and wondered what I was supposed to do. I took in a deep breath and followed him in to the living room. This whole wing was his suite it seemed. I spotted Tyler and Steele relaxing on the plush oversized couch. They were absorbed in the show they watched and it piqued my interest. On the massive flat-screen was Rocket Power. I hadn't seen that cartoon in years, and even then it was re-runs. I almost laughed out loud at their choice of show, and at how the three cartoon characters could very well be these three assholes. My eyes caught Hawke's as he looked at me puzzled. He nodded for me to follow him. I walked past the two on the couch and into an office-looking room, only it wasn't an office, it was more like the FBI surveillance headquarters.

"Holy shit," I blurted, as my eyes scanned the room. Numerous computer screens took up one entire wall. It looked like a state-of-the-art security system.

"Welcome to Hawke headquarters." Hawke admired his endless computer screens, monitors, and gaming consoles.

"More like dork quarters." Steele entered the room and tapped something into one of the keyboards to fire up a live camera.

"You're just jealous you're all brawn and no brain," Hawke joked and joined Steele in peering at the screen.

Was that the secret party club location? It

looked all too familiar, but I couldn't put my finger on where it was. Underneath the wall of computers was a narrow desk, which ran along the entire wall, with three swivel chairs pushed underneath. In the middle of the room was a large mahogany table with four black leather-bound chairs. In the center of the table sat one of those ugly ass skull globe things. A plush couch was nestled against the wall, adjacent to the table, and a small bar was set up next to it. "Are we working in here?" I looked at their backs and wondered what they were up to.

"I'll go get some pants on, it will probably help you concentrate better." Hawke winked at me and disappeared.

After a long, tense silence, Steele turned to eye me suspiciously. His arms were crossed over his broad chest and he cocked his head to the side. "You surprise me, Bambi."

"How so?" I was curious to see what he had to say.

"You've kept your mouth shut, even though you know more of our business than any other outsider."

"It's not my place to tell your secrets," I said

evenly. Where was he going with this?

"Even so, you've every right to spill. Not that it would do you any good." His eyes caught me in their web.

"Look Steele, I'm here to finish senior year. Get into a good college, as far away from the East coast as possible, and forget my past. I don't want to get in your way, or anyone's as a matter of fact. What you and the other two Stooge's do in your spare time is none of my business."

He gave me a questioning look, as though he tried to dissect the meaning behind my words. He went to leave but then hesitated in the doorway. "Don't think you've scored any brownie points for keeping your mouth shut." He glanced back at me, but the look in his eyes had changed. Gone was his usual dark glare and in its place was something less sinister.

I pulled out one of the leather chairs and sat my grungy ass down. I felt out of place in here, with my crappy looking clothing. Oh well, I was only here to finish this damned assignment. I pulled out my phone, workbook, laptop, and pens and started to jot down an outline.

Hawke returned and placed a can of coke on the table in front of me. He threw a bag of crisps and a bag of gummi bears on the table before he grabbed his laptop and sat in the chair next to mine. I was grateful he had put on a shirt too. I didn't think I would have been able to concentrate in close quarters with him half-naked.

"So, what's the plan?" He threw a handful of gummi bears into his mouth and I tried with all my strength not to watch his mouth as he chewed.

"I've written down all the events in chronological order. Let's pick half each and re-write from Lady McBeth's point of view, and concentrate on how we perceived her." I glanced up at him.

He narrowed his eyes at me. "I'll do the first half, you do the second. Then we'll swap and edit each other's work to make it seem like it was written by one person," he added.

"Okay." I was impressed, but I didn't want him to know that. I underestimated his work ethic and was pleasantly surprised he wanted to put in the effort. I got to work and had my half of the assignment completed within the hour. We'd both sat in silence the whole time, too busy to chat or make any small talk.

"Want to take a break?" Hawke asked. He leaned back in his chair, placed his hands behind his head and stretched out his neck muscles. My eyes followed his movements and I had the urge to run my tongue up the side of his elongated neck, to feel the smooth skin against my lips.

I cleared my throat. "Sounds good." I watched him stand and head out of the room. I was going to sit in the room until he came back, but his voice made me jump.

"You coming, Bambi?" he called over the noise of the cartoon.

I closed my eyes and counted to three before I hauled ass into the other room. The three of them were sprawled out over the couch and they'd left a big enough space for me to join them. Tyler and Hawke were practically sitting on each other, and Tyler patted the space on the other side of him for me to sit.

"I never would have pictured you three watching Rocket Power." I climbed over Steele's legs and planted myself between him and Tyler, thankful for the large space I had.

Tyler and Steele leaned into me then and reached their hands toward each other so they hovered over my lap.

"Woogity, woogity," they hollered in unison as they wiggled their fingers at one another.

"You guys are insane." I burst out laughing and pushed their hands away from me.

"You can't say this isn't the best cartoon ever made in the history of all cartoons." Tyler moved back and draped his arm around Hawke's shoulders.

"Nope, nothing beats Rugrats." I was very aware of Steele still being so close. I felt the hairs on my arms prickle at the thought of him touching my skin.

"That's such a girl thing to say." Tyler pushed my shoulder and I fell into Steele. I shot Tyler a glare and he winked back at me, knowing exactly what he was doing.

I moved back into a sitting position and crossed my legs under me.

"So, Bambi. What pizza do you like?" Steele scrolled on his phone.

"I um, I don't mind. I'm not staying that long. We got our drafts finished so I'll head home soon." I tried to sound calm and collected, but my tone came out harsh.

"Relax, we're only eating pizza and watching cartoons. Think you can un-serious yourself sometimes?" Steele turned to look at me, his cocky grin made me clench my hands together.

"That's not even a word." I rolled my eyes.

"My point exactly," he chuckled. "Well, I've ordered four different types, so hopefully one, or all, will be to your satisfaction." He licked his lips and it made my insides do somersaults.

I quickly turned my attention back to the screen and sat silent until Steele got up and sauntered out of the room. I felt like I could breathe all of a sudden, without all three of them around me. I glanced over at Tyler and Hawke, they seemed so comfortable around one another and I wondered if they were together at all? I mean, after their hot display at the secret party, I wouldn't mind one bit if they decided to repeat it.

"What's going on in that pretty little head of yours?" Tyler sat forward and grabbed a can of coke off the coffee table.

"Nothing at all," I lied and watched his lips

as they connected with the can. I was reminded of those lips on me and I refocused on the cartoon to try to quell the thoughts.

"Hope you're all hungry," Steele announced as he entered the room.

The delicious smell of fresh pizza hit me and I realized I was starving. One slice wouldn't hurt, would it? The guys' casual and normal behavior had me on edge. My stomach ached and I wasn't entirely convinced it was because of my hunger pangs. I watched them as they all grabbed a piece and settled back into the couch like this was a regular Friday night hang-out session. It was weird. They demolished a whole pizza each and then polished off the last of the fourth pizza. I was dumbfounded that they could decimate four pizzas in such a short amount of time. I'd eaten four slices in the time it took them to eat the rest.

"Anyone want dessert?" Hawke jumped up and stretched.

"Fuck yes!" Both Steele and Tyler high-fived over my head.

"You staying, Bambi?" Tyler glanced at me.

"Thanks, but I think I should get home." I

stood and headed into Hawke's computer room and gathered my things together. The whole evening was off. I couldn't work out why they were all of sudden so normal and not being total assholes to me. My instincts told me to leave while everything was still smooth sailing.

I emerged from the room with no sign of Hawke anymore. "Thanks for the pizza. Tell Hawke I'll email him my half of the assignment." I said as I scurried out and before I was convinced to stay. I found my way downstairs, and out the back of the house, with no sight of Hawke. It was fucking freezing, and the whip of cold air that hit me at all angles, made my teeth chatter.

I nearly went ass up, down the dunes, but managed to catch myself before I face planted. I was confident the guys weren't going to follow me, but I hurried my pace as I was freezing my tits off. I crossed my arms over my chest to try to keep myself warm, not paying any attention to how dark it was out here. The moon was hidden behind the thick cloud and the ocean looked as though Ursula had painted it with her squid ink.

I froze when I sensed something or someone, behind me, hidden in the dunes. I turned around and stared into the darkness as my heart pounded in my chest. Nothing but the howl of the wind and the movement of the tall grass caught my attention. I was fucking losing it.

I trudged on, my shoes now filled with cold sand, as I stopped being careful how I stepped. I just wanted to get home and out of the cold.

Fuck.

I paused my footsteps to listen and narrowed my senses to what I thought were footsteps.

"I know it's one of you guys," I shouted at the dunes.

No response.

Shit. My mind was playing with me. I closed my eyes for a brief moment, took in a deep calming breath, and headed back along the beach. I tried to ignore the thump of my heart in my ears.

A sharp pain splintered through my skull, and a flash of light danced across my eyes, as I fell onto my hands and knees onto the soft bed of sand. I choked out a cry and clawed at the night, as black spots danced across my vision, and my eyes began to close. I circled in on myself when I felt blow after blow hit me in the stomach, the pain searing my insides until finally the dark ink of the ocean overtook me and drifted me to unconsciousness.

Chapter Nineteen

Peyton

I came to with my arms pinned above my head. My shoulders were stiff and sore from their position as his strong fingers held me in place and cut off my circulation. I struggled under his weight and this only excited him more as his fingernails dug into my flesh. I concentrated on the pain, on the deep ache in my bones, and the sharp sting as his nails bit into my skin.

"There you are, my sweet girl. You know I don't like you unconscious." He breathed against my neck.

I'd been here before. This was all too familiar. I tried to let my mind wander to somewhere else but this time it felt different. I didn't dare open my eyes. If I kept my eyes closed, I could pretend this was just a fucking nightmare. But the weight of his body reminded me of exactly where I was and of what was about to happen. I struggled to breathe as the pressure pushed down on my bruised ribs. Fuck, I think one was broken, the sharp pain gave me something else to focus on other than the nightmare in front of me. The familiar scent of him made my insides coil and bile rise to my throat. The cold seeped through my bones and the press of the concrete floor against my flesh made me want to scream.

I felt him shift and he whispered soft kisses across my neck and over my shoulder. A repulsive shiver snaked its way across my skin, exposing me. Only, he thought this was from arousal and I heard his appreciative moan as his mouth moved back up and hovered over my ear.

"I missed you, baby Blue." His sick voice filled my ears.

I pulled my head away from him and

scrunched my eyes tighter, drawing away into my head like I'd done countless times before. I could feel the fuzz drop over my consciousness allowing me a sweet reprieve from what I knew was to come.

"Don't be like that. I know you've missed me too. I can tell by the way you respond to my touch." His lips moved against my skin.

I tensed under him and held my breath as his teeth connected with the sensitive skin on my neck. He bit me, and I did all I could to not jerk away from him. He liked it when I struggled and tried to escape him. It fed his sick and abhorrent mind. His bulge sat between my legs and twitched and I knew he got off on inflicting pain. I had been his favorite toy to play with. To do as he pleased with, no matter the severity of the injuries he dished out. I tried to forget the time he had one of the girls tied up, her battered and bruised body not enough to make him stop. She wouldn't cum for him, she was barely conscious at this point and I'd had been ordered to watch as he sliced her nipples off and stuffed them in his pocket. He was a monster to the others. I guessed I could thank my lucky stars I was his favorite.

"Did you miss me?" He licked the entire left side of my face and made my skin crawl. "I'm supposed to take you back. But I'm a little selfish, Blue. I want to keep you all for myself. I don't want to share you anymore." His lips vibrated against the side of my face.

He enjoyed every minute of his torture and pretended like his gentle touches made up for his pain. I felt his grip loosen on my wrists as he transferred his steel grip from both my wrists to his one hand and traced the other one down the side of my body. He snaked his dirty hand inside of my pants until he reached between my legs and shoved three fingers roughly inside me. I whimpered in pain as his fingernails scraped against my insides. The unwanted intrusion of him made me squirm and he let out an animalistic groan as he pumped his fingers roughly into me. Another part of my soul fractured as the reality hit that I was back here. The pieces of myself I'd managed to claw back since he last did this, were slowly being torn away from me again.

"You like that don't you, Blue. You like it when I hurt you. You like it when I make your cunt bleed, my dirty girl." He ran his nose over my jaw and breathed me in.

My nausea churned in my stomach and acidic bile rose up my throat and threatened to explode out of me as his lips moved to hover over my mouth. He placed slow tender kisses on my sealed lips as though he savored every second of his torture. I couldn't turn my face far enough away from him to stop his tongue as it licked my mouth and tasted me.

"Give into me, baby." He forced his tongue inside my mouth and I gagged as his stiff bulge pressed into me harder.

I swallowed thickly and panic seized me at this point and I knew what I had to do. I forced my mind into a state of nothingness and made myself a shell to be used as they conditioned me to do. I knew the only way I could distract him was if he thought he had broken me again. I pushed my hips back into him and met him thrust for thrust, the sharp stabbing pain in my ribs sent waves of nausea through me. I had to grit my teeth together to stop the cry of pain that I wanted so badly to let out.

"That's it, dirty girl, you know how I like it. Soon I'll have my cock buried deep inside your dirty cunt." He whispered against my lips and bit down until I could feel the warmth of my blood trickle down my cheek. His fingers slid out of me and his hand found its way to my ass cheek. I knew I had him at this point. He was too far into this and soon would be overtaken by his needs.

I opened my eyes and stared up at him. He looked exactly the same as the last time I'd seen him, only now he sported a fresh black eye. His dark hair was styled to perfection and his sharp jaw slacked as his arousal intensified. I lifted my legs and wrapped them around his waist and held him firm against me.

He moaned and licked the blood as it trickled over my cheek. "The fucking things you do to me."

His hand loosened and let go of my wrists, and left behind scorched skin where his hands had me in a tight grip. I knew he'd thought he'd won, that he'd finally broken me again and I wouldn't fight back. He'd done this enough times to know what I could endure and that I could never fight long enough to keep him off. The cool air did nothing to soothe the pain and I tried to focus on his movements. I moved my stiff arms and wrapped them around his neck as he gripped my ass in both his hands. His fingernails dug into my flesh and would leave crescent-shaped marks no doubt. His eyes softened as he watched me respond to his touch. "Your cunt is my obsession, Blue. Don't fucking deny me it for this long, again." He buried his face into my neck and sucked my skin into his mouth.

I slid my hand down his back and reached for my knife that I'd thankfully strapped above my ankle before I headed to Hawke's. I continued to rub his neck with my other hand to keep him from noticing my movements, knowing it would work as he'd conditioned me to give him small touches to make him feel wanted. He shifted and I froze as panic reared inside me, the thought of not being able to end this weighed heavily on my heart. He dragged my track pants down over my ass and groaned as his hand wedged between us to grip his bulge. I felt the tip press against me and a hiss escaped his lips as he adjusted himself.

"You'll never fucking have me again, you sick fuck." I gritted through clenched teeth and brought my knife down hard into his side. The blade slid through his ribs and I was surprised I had managed to line it up right. I jerked it back out and plunged it in again.

A roar of agony ripped out of his mouth and he hovered over me for a moment, long enough for me to pull the blade out of his flesh and swing my arm to pierce his throat. A twisted and strangled cry filled the cold air as his red-rimmed eyes focused on my face. Blood had started to pulsate out of his throat where my knife still sat firmly embedded in his flesh. I watched him change color and blood splattered from his mouth and sprayed over me. He began to slacken and I was barely able to hold him up off me, but I watched in satisfaction as his life bled out of him.

"Go to hell." I tried to push his dead weight to the side when a deafening thump pierced the otherwise still air.

My heart dropped. Fuck. Were the others here too? Did they come looking for me to drag me back? There was no way in hell I was getting shipped back to Black Grove River, they'd have to kill me first. My heart thrummed in my chest, the sound of it vibrated through my ears, as I managed to squirm out from under the fucker's limp body and roll to my side. A nauseating pain shot through me and I curled into a ball to ride out the wave of agony. I knew I had to get the fuck out of wherever I was and I knew I had to be quick. I glanced around and the dim light that streamed in from the rag-covered windows revealed I was in some sort of abandoned warehouse. Fucking great.

The door I faced flew off its hinges and crashed to the floor in an ear-splitting boom. I flinched when three figures stormed into the warehouse, their demeanor all too familiar. I wanted to crawl away from them. I wanted to move but the pain was unbearable.

"Over here." One called as he jogged over to where I lay on the ground.

I watched him take in the scene, his eyes danced between my dead attacker and me, unable to form words. "I'm okay." I choked out while holding my arm protectively over my ribs.

Tyler squatted down and reached a hand out to hover over my arm. He didn't touch me, he knew I wouldn't want any form of human contact at this point. "What the fuck, Bambi? Are you okay?" His eyes landed on my bare ass and he hoisted my pants back up.

I was so grateful for him right then, for his simple act of kindness. "He didn't." I closed my eyes for a moment to take in my words. The fucker wouldn't try to fucking break me ever again.

Steele strode up to stand next to Tyler, he surveyed the scene before him before he lifted his boot and kicked my now dead attacker away from me. "Lucky you left your phone on the desk at Hawke's or we would have never found you." He glanced at me and back at the dead fucker. "I'm fucking impressed, Bambi." He looked at me with adoration for a split second, then his usual steel façade was back.

"What?" I looked up at them confused.

Tyler rubbed the back of his neck and shot Steele a look before he held his hands out for me to grip.

I let him haul me carefully to a sitting position when Hawke approached us. His eyes were wary and hid a glint of darkness behind them. "You okay?" He stood and stared at my dead attacker.

"How did you all find me?" I braced my hand against the cold concrete floor to hold myself up.

"Steele put a tracker on your phone." Hawke fessed up.

"Shouldn't leave your shit lying around at other people's places." Steele narrowed his eyes at me.

I almost laughed at him. He was still so indifferent but in a caring way. "Thank you." I looked up at him and he nodded in return. "Under normal circumstances, I'd have kicked your ass."

Steele snorted and stepped around me to nudge the dead guy with his boot. "We'll deal with this. Get her home, Tyler."

"Let's get you out of here." Tyler slowly placed his arm around my back and helped me to my feet. "Can you walk?" He kept his arm around me for support.

"Of course, I can. It's only a few broken ribs. I've had worse." I glanced up at him.

I heard Steele's and Hawke's hushed voices as they discussed what they planned for my attacker. I wasn't entirely sure but I thought one of them had mentioned an acid drum. We stepped through the doorway into blaring daylight. "What time is it?" I squinted into the sun.

"Just after nine in the morning." Tyler led me to Steele's black Maserati and opened the door for me.

I managed to sit in the car without causing myself too much pain. "Hey, do you mind finding my bag?"

"On it." Tyler jogged back into the warehouse and emerged within seconds and handed me my bag.

"Thanks." He closed the door on me and climbed into the driver's seat, leaned his head back, and shut his eyes.

He kept his eyes closed as he spoke. "Capri called me this morning looking for you. When I tapped into your phone, I knew you were in trouble." He opened his eyes and his burning gaze met mine. "I'm so fucking sorry we didn't get here quicker."

I watched him grip the steering wheel, his knuckles turned white as he peeled out of the warehouse parking lot. He didn't utter another word, he didn't glance my way and his company didn't make me feel uncomfortable.

After all that I had endured, I felt safe with him, with all of them. Somewhere along the way, these guys managed to filter into my brain and unlock a small part of me that was willing to trust again. "It's not your fault. That fucker in there is from my past," I sighed.

I'd hoped to never face my past again, to keep my new life separate. But, here they both were, colliding like a fucking freight train. My phone buzzed and I leaned forward, forgetting the excruciating pain in my ribs, I choked out a small grunt as I riffled through my bag for my phone. I glanced at the screen. It was almost out of charge and saw numerous texts and millions of missed calls. I quickly fired off a text to Capri to put her at ease and then scrolled until his name jumped out at me.

Dylan: *Blue, don't make me do this the hard way.*

I stared at his message. It was sent last night at 9 o'clock. No message followed. I replied with all I could think to write. Three words.

Me: *He found me.*

I shut off my phone screen and hoped that was the end of the conversation. The end of that chapter. My phone vibrated in my hand. I swallowed the lump in my throat and opened the screen back up.

Dylan: *They sent him.*

My stomach bottomed out and my phone slid from my tingling fingers. It landed on my thigh and fell to the car floor. I could barely breathe, the claustrophobic cabin of the car made my anxiety worse. I tried to swallow the thick saliva as it pooled in my mouth, but it made me gasp for air. I opened the window and let the wind blow over my face. It didn't help. I could feel my attack start to build deep in my chest. The dull ache spread quickly as my heart picked up speed. My fingers and lips became numb and I tried to concentrate on my counting. It was fucking useless in instances like this when an attack threatened your sanity and rendered you useless.

"Are you okay?" Tyler worried.

"No, I'm not." I breathed through pursed lips. "I feel like I'm going to pass out." I shook my hands erratically to try to get feeling back.

"Here, give me your hand." Tyler reached across and grabbed my hand closest to him. "Freak out all you want. I've got you here with me. I'll keep you here." He gripped my hand tightly and it was the firm pressure that made me start to come back down from my attack.

"I'm sorry." I apologized and rested my head back and breathed in deeply as I held his hand. I could feel the sweat start to bead on my forehead and I knew I would be okay, I just needed a few more minutes to calm myself.

"Don't apologize. It's okay." He squeezed my hand as he drove into our driveway.

The dead fucker hadn't taken me far, he'd stopped at the nearby industrial estate. The thought of him watching me while I was unconscious made my stomach coil and my anger stir deep within. I hoped that Steele and Hawke made his body disappear forever, never to be found again.

I stared out the window at the house as Tyler put the car in park. "Please don't tell anyone about this." My voice was small and I was ashamed of how they had found me.

Tyler's hand, still firmly wrapped around mine, gave me a small squeeze of understanding. "Whatever you want, Peyton. Just know I'm here for you." With that, he let go of my hand and waited for me to respond.

I couldn't look him in the eyes, I didn't want to see his pity aimed at me. "Thanks," I said as I grabbed my bag and managed to climb out and close the car door after me. My body ached like a bitch but it was nothing compared to what could have been. I'd endured much, much worse at the hands of that fucker when I was back in their clasps. His disappearance wouldn't go unnoticed and I'd have to face the consequences eventually.

I heard the window as it opened. "I'll check in later," Tyler called out after me.

I turned around and gave him a small smile. It was all I could muster up for him. I wanted to thank him and the other two but I didn't know how. What they did for me this morning, I could never repay in favors, but I was damned sure they would come collect soon.

After the Spanish Inquisition from Capri and her bawling her eyes out on me for not being there to stop what had happened, I headed to my bathroom and peeled my soiled clothing off. I threw them straight in a trash bag and never wanted to look at them again. I climbed into my bath and soaked my weary bones until the water cooled. I had purple bruises to one side of me and the place on my lip where the fucker had bitten me was swollen. I'd cleaned up my wound with an antiseptic wash and applied some antiseptic cream to help it heal. I knew I was safe from him, they all had routine monthly testing done so they could continue with their abhorrent and vile ways. The thought made me shudder.

After I dried off and got dressed in oversized pajamas, I climbed into bed, put in my earbuds to listen to Eminem as I tried to sleep the rest of the day away.

I woke to the buzz of my phone next to my head. I looked at the time and it was midday. I'd slept the whole night and the morning. I eased myself up and flinched at the sharp pain in my side. That was going to take a while to heal. I checked my phone again. A new message from Dylan was at the top of the list. I sighed as I clicked on it, knowing all too well what was coming.

Dylan: *You owe Dev. It's safer if I bring you back.*

Me: *I'm not going back.*

He sent through photos of the fucker who had attacked me. His chopped-up body was stuffed into a drum with his severed head resting on top. I threw my phone onto the bed and couldn't work out how he had those photos. It had only been a day since I'd left Hawke and Steele behind. Fuck. How did they know The Black Grove Chapter? Nausea settled in my stomach and I wanted to hurl up my guts. How the fuck was I going to fix this? Why were the guys messaging those ruthless fuckers back home?

My phone chimed again and I was almost too scared to pick it up. I held my breath as I opened his text. A photo of me passed out in the back of some unknown car, in my red dress from the party, popped up on my screen. My heart lurched at the image. What type of sick person would do this? Who the fuck had these photos? Another message popped up. A photo of my mom and Nathaniel, enjoying lunch wherever they were on holiday.

Me: *Who sent you these?*

I was ready to flee again. To leave my mom behind to keep her safe. My phone buzzed and my eyes unwillingly slid to the screen.

Dylan: *Looks like you've got yourself tangled up amongst The Brotherhood of the*

Skulls. Dev is fuming.

I read over his text a few times and tried to work out what the fuck he was on about. The mention of Dev, short for Devil, had me backtrack. That man sent cold fear through the most ruthless men. I'd seen his soldiers kneel before him and take an oath only to be shot in the head at the next gathering for not meeting their quota or for simply being late. Dev didn't take prisoners. He took lives. Once you were in, you were his. It was why I understood how Dylan couldn't just leave. He'd signed his soul to the Devil and almost lost it when I ran.

I gripped my phone in my shaking hand. If Dev ordered my return, Dylan would have to stop at nothing to make it happen. Just like the dead fucker who was now disintegrating in a barrel of acid. He was one of Dev's best clients and now that Dev knew the fucker was dead, he was going to make me pay big time.

"Fuck!" I screamed at the top of my lungs and threw my phone across the room like a spoiled brat.

Capri rushed in, lucky it was only the two of us home, my mom and Nathaniel still blissfully away on their extended business vacation. "Are you okay?" She stopped mid-step when she saw my face.

"Shit has hit the fan." I held my face in my hands.

Capri sat down next to me and held a bowl of freshly made pasta under my nose. She knew food fixed everything usually, but I wasn't sure anything could fix this massive fuck up. "You need to eat."

I took the bowl from her and my stomach grumbled in appreciation. "Thanks for looking after me." I glanced at her and smiled.

She raised her eyebrows and shoved a mouthful of pasta in her mouth and then handed me the fork. "Eat."

I scooped the pasta up and eyed the shape of them. "Is this penis pasta?" I turned the fork around in front of my face to get a better angle.

"No fucking idea where it came from, but it was the only pasta I could find." She shrugged.

I burst out laughing. "Ouch." I flinched as the pain in my ribs pinched.

"Serves you right for laughing at my cooking skills." Capri giggled. "Just eat the fucking pasta, we both know you like dick in the mouth."

I shook my head. "I can't believe you just said that." I shoveled in a forkful and it was delicious. I chewed slowly so I wouldn't split open the bite mark on my lip.

Capri left me to eat my pasta and disappeared into her room. I could hear the sounds of music float down the hall and I knew she was worried. Capri always played her music extra loud when she was stressed. I climbed off my bed and placed my empty bowl on my desk and snuck a look at the pool house, wondering if Colton was in there, if he knew of the recent events. My mind reeled on the whole Brotherhood of the Skulls Dylan had mentioned in his text. Was it the same as the one Colton had punished me for mentioning? My skin heated at the thought of that night, me on my knees and his relentless thrusts.

My door swung open and Capri stormed in with a look of horror plastered on her face. "Have you looked at your phone?"

I shook my head. "No, why?"

"Fuck, Pey! Fuck!" She started to pace my room. "This is fucking bad."

"What are you talking about?" I followed her

movements.

She stopped suddenly and held her phone out to me and scrunched her eyes closed. "This."

I walked closer to get a better look and lost the feeling in my legs. I slumped to the floor and lay back with my arm over my eyes to stop the image from replaying in my head.

"Peyton." Capri tried to pry my arm from my eyes. "Peyton!" She sat down next to me.

"Fuck." I groaned and wanted to melt into the floor and disappear.

"Nice choice of words." Capri laughed.

I pulled my arm off my face and glared at her. "So not a time for laughter. Show me again." I took her phone from her and watched the GIF some fucker had made of me and Colton in the stationery room. My head was flung back in ecstasy while my skirt sat around my waist. At least you couldn't entirely tell it was Colton, unless you focused on his neck tattoo. The bastards made a border of blue dicks around it and when I looked at the name of who posted it, I nearly died. Fucking Steele Manning. Why the hell would he do this? They fucking played me, making me think they were decent human beings when in fact they were the total opposite. I couldn't believe I'd let my guard down and managed to get blindsided by those fuckers. They were all probably laughing their asses off at my expense.

Capri pulled the phone from me and shut the screen off. "It'll blow over before you know it." She tried to reassure me.

"I could fucking kill him." I struggled to sit up without being in pain. "I'm going over to his place right now. We're going to end this shit." I breathed heavily as I climbed to my knees and stood.

Capri looked up at me. "They're all gone away." She sympathized.

"Gone away," I repeated.

"Mm-hm."

"How fucking convenient. I wonder if Colton has seen this?" I walked to the balcony and glared down at the pool house.

"He's with them." She whispered.

I gripped the railing, my knuckles turned white from my anger, and the rage within me burned like lava ready to erupt. "Of course he is." I turned on the spot and looked at Capri.

"You know what, fuck them all." I stormed into my room and pulled Capri off the floor. "We're going shopping."

CHAPTER TWENTY

Peyton

Capri and I had spent the night holed up inside, doing girly things and enjoying having the whole house to ourselves. Mom and Nathaniel were away for another two weeks, their business trip turned into a holiday. Colton was off with his fucking mates doing who knows what.

It was early morning before school as we sat in Capri's Mercedes. I stared at my reflection in the mirror, a version of me I hadn't encountered before glared back at me with steel resolve. My freshly dyed sky blue hair matched the storm that brewed in my eyes. The same blue as the wig I wore when Devil made me perform. The same blue as Steele's fucking eyes. This was an ode to him and his inability to break me, as he had promised.

"Ready?" I cocked an eyebrow at Capri, who looked back at me with equal parts of concern and admiration.

"Are you sure you want to do this?" She grabbed my hand in hers and squeezed it.

"Fucking oath." I peeled myself out of Capri's car and held my bag in one hand, with the zipper undone. I glanced down at my newly improved uniform. From my Doc Martens and ripped stockings, to my extra short skirt and untucked school shirt that now gaped across my breasts. If these snobby St. Ivy students were going to depict me as a slut, I'd wear the motherfucking crown and own it.

It was like the first day all over again, but now the students of St. Ivy really had something to gawk at. As we headed up toward the main building, I heard their snickers and whispered insults. I smiled at each and every one of them as I handed them a knitted blue dick keyring. They all looked at me horrified, and didn't know what to do with themselves as they took my little gift. Fuck them all.

Capri and I had knitted little blue dicks and attached keychains, so I could give one to each person who made a stupid fucking comment. My way of owning my mistake and not letting these fucking preppy bitches get the upper hand.

Capri grabbed my hand firmly in hers as we waited at the entry doors, a gentle squeeze let me know she was here for me. I handed each student a dick as they arrived and topped it off with a big ass grin. Some looked at me as though I'd grown two heads, and those were the students I knew hadn't seen the stupid GIF.

"Hey, Peyton, want to fuck me in the Janitor's room," a senior guy shouted across the hall, his accomplished grin made my nostrils flare.

"No one's going to fuck you, moron," Capri shouted back and I glanced at her in thanks.

I ignored him and made my way down the long hall, with Capri by my side, as I handed out the remaining dicks to everyone that passed me. They either said thanks or eyed me in disgust. I was beyond giving a shit what these fuckers thought of me, and this was probably the last time I'd see them anyway. I brushed off their scrutiny and strutted my short skirt down the hall.

We approached my locker and I stared at it for a few moments before I entered my keycode to unlocked it. Sitting front and center was an envelope. The same black one Owen had received in class. "What the fuck is this?" I plucked it up in my fingers and ripped it open.

"Oh, fuck," Capri sighed.

The shiny black card had the same symbol on it as the card I'd received my first day, however, the scrawl on the back was different.

Mors tua, vita mea.

"What the fuck does that even mean?" I threw it back in my locker.

"They're like a game or something. I don't know." Capri shrugged, as she scanned the hallway.

I grabbed out my phone from my bag, closed my eyes for a few beats, and sucked in a grounding breath. No time to change my mind now. I hesitated for a spilt second before I placed my phone on top of the dumb card with the skull on it, and slammed my locker shut. My eyes flitted to Capri, and I swallowed the lump that had formed in my throat all of a sudden. "You know I love you and you're my soul sister."

She looked at me concerned. "Why does this feel like it's something more?"

"Shush, and give me a hug." I gripped her around the shoulders and squeezed her into me. The sharp sting of my broken ribs reminded me of what was to come. "Thanks for always having my back."

"Right back at you, baby." She leaned in and kissed my cheek before unwrapping her arms from around my waist.

"I have one last special delivery." I waggled my eyebrows.

"I can't wait to see his face tonight," Capri laughed, and slapped my ass as I strode away from her and toward the faculty building.

I felt the judgement from the other students as they eyeballed my new look. The obvious disgust they emanated, slid right off me as I strutted through the elite St. Ivy halls. I doubted this school had ever seen a student rebel and go against the strict uniform policy.

It was still quite early and I knew Colton wouldn't have been here yet. That was if he'd returned from his boy's getaway, but none the less, my heart still hammered as I neared his office. It was empty. I took a slow glance around to catalogue every last inch of his office in my brain. His masculine scent lingered and I wondered how long he was going to be away for. I ran my finger over the hardwood of his desk and images of Stass bent over it, flooded my mind. Rage simmered in my veins at the thought and I chided myself for allowing my mind to go there.

I pulled out the last knitted dick and placed it in the middle of his desk. I wondered if he'd show his face today, not that anyone knew it was him, apart from the fucker who took the video. On that thought, I exited his office and closed the door behind me.

I marched through the school and flipped off anyone that made faces at me. I was so done with them all. As I rounded the corner of the front gates, I stopped dead in my tracks. There he was. All broody, tattooed, and dangerous. He looked even bigger than the last time I'd seen him. If that was even possible. Dylan straddled his motorbike and rested his helmet in front of him. His eyes caught mine, and he cocked an eyebrow as he took in my new uniform.

"Well, look what the cat dragged out of her preppy school. What's with the uniform?" His gaze dragged over me ever so fucking slowly.

"Don't start," I huffed and pulled the straps of my bag over both of my shoulders.

"You know, it's better this way. If I take you back, you're under my protection." The furrow between his eyebrows deepened at that revelation.

I grabbed the helmet from the back of the bike and watched his eyes turn to slits. "Like I have a fucking choice," I seethed. The fact that I'd been summoned, made no difference to anyone but me. I would have had my dead ass dragged back there whether I wanted to go or not.

"Here comes trouble," Dylan said, a sinister growl etched into his tone. His icy gaze cut to me before he slammed his helmet on and revved the motorbike.

I turned around, only to lock eyes with Steele. His hard glare penetrated right through me and I could see his rage as it simmered in his eyes, mercilessly cold and calculating. He didn't move an inch as we stared at each other. Hawke and Tyler flanked him, and both their cold gazes bounced between me and Dylan. I couldn't believe I'd let my guard down and trusted them. After the relatively normal study hang out and the fucked up events that followed, I thought we'd turned a corner. Nothing too extreme, but I'd thought we'd all had an unspoken mutual truce. What a fucking gullible idiot I had become.

"Let's just go." I swung my leg over and straddled the bike. I pressed against Dylan's back, and a hiss escaped my lips as the sharp sting cut into my ribs. I sliced my eyes over to the three of them as they stood there and watched me. I made sure to connect my glare with Steele's one last time, to let him know I wasn't done with him. Anger burned in my veins and hatred bubbled in my chest as I slammed the helmet on my head and wrapped my arms around Dylan's waist. The Ducati roared out of the school grounds, leaving my tormentors behind and taking me back to my nightmares.

EPILOGUE

Peyton

My chest rose and fell as I stared down at the fucker at my feet. His lifeless body was sprawled out on the marble floor with his dick laying limp in his hand. Blood. There was so much fucking blood. It was painted over my body and his, in a spectacular mess.

Fuck.

It wasn't supposed to happen like this.

I ran my shaking hand over the cuts he slashed across my skin.

I'm going to stab you, Blue, and then fuck the holes until I fill you up and my cum oozes out everywhere.

His sick voice still rang in my ears.

Fuck. Fuck. Fuck.

I padded across the opulent room and searched in my bag for my phone. I fished it out and nearly dropped it thanks to the uncontrollable tremble of my hands.

I felt my whole body begin to numb and I knew I was on the verge of a panic attack. I quickly dressed in my robe and waited patiently for him to come fix my mess.

Me: *It's done.*

Dylan: *That's my girl.*

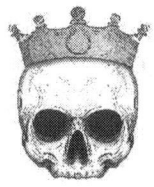

Author's Note

Thank you ever so much for reading Corrupt Temptation, book 1 in the Savage Kings of St. Ivy series. I hope you enjoyed getting to know Peyton and her guys as much as I enjoyed writing their story. If you need to know what happens next, make sure you one-click Savage Lies.

I wanted to thank my amazing readers for this journey you are taking with me. For reading my books and making my dreams come true. It means the world to me that you support my work. Without you all, I wouldn't have the chance to live my dream.

A special thank you goes to all the people who have kept me sane and on track until the end. I'm so thankful for each of you. To all those that I have endlessly annoyed to read my shitty first drafts (Danni, I'm looking at you) and to all those that have stuck around. You guys are my people! To my Beta Queens, my Booknerds and my Boss Babes, thank you for your endless support and shouting from the rooftops and getting excited with each new release.

Much love

Melinda Terranova
xoxox

BOOKS BY MELINDA

Savage Kings of St. Ivy

Corrupt Temptation

Savage Lies

Verona Academy

Cruel Summer

Vicious Enzo

New York Princess

Heir of the Blood Curse Series

Bequeathed

Blood Prince

STALK ME

Join my Facebook Group:
www.facebook.com/groups/MelsBooknerds

Stalk me on Facebook:
www.facebook.com/MelindaTerranovaAuthor

Stalk me on Instagram:
www.instagram.com/melinda.terranova.author

Website:www.melindaterranova.com

Printed in Great Britain
by Amazon

87869663R00194